MATED TO THE PRIDE

JADE ALTERS

BLAKE

Our pride's workout routine was always punishing, but never more so than the few weeks before a big mission. Now that there were only ten days before we left for our latest engagement, I was holding nothing back. As alpha commander, senior both in our pride and our military actions, it was my responsibility to keep these men alive.

Of course, I did that in many different ways — but keeping them in peak physical condition definitely wouldn't hurt.

I paced my breathing as I continued on the rowing machine, pushing hard to meet the same high bar I'd set for the others. Sure, we stuck to traditional pride hierarchy like any other group of shifters, but our work bound us together. I was their leader, but also their equal. I never asked them to do anything I wouldn't do myself.

"You okay there, chief?"

I paused to look across at the speaker. If I wasn't pushing my body so hard, Hale's grin would be as infectious as always. Of the entire pride, it was Hale that had the most feline energy in this form. His dark, narrow eyes were intense and focused, playful as he was. Outsiders tended to find him intimidating and were surprised to learn that nobody in our group agreed — especially since Hale was also my second-in-command.

I shot him a look back. "I'm fine."

"I don't know. You got some heavy breathing going on over there."

I shook my head. I was too focused to smile, but Hale knew me well enough to read it in my eyes. "Focus on yourself, smart-ass. You sure you haven't turned down the resistance?"

"I just want everyone to know," said Hale, turning around to face Stone and Preston, "that our fearless leader is accusing me of slacking off."

"Uh-huh," said Preston. He wasn't much of a talker, but he didn't have to be. The smirk he shot back at Hale did all the talking for him. Strangers tended to be confused by that. They hadn't learned to pick up on his signals like we had and saw him as a mystery man. An enigma. The piercings in his upper ear and eyebrow likely helped that along — as well as his sleek wave of dark hair, dashed with a fleck of premature silver. Preston was only 28, and looked it. The little gray looked curious, and often had people joking that we put him through too much stress.

"If only he could accuse you of shutting up," said Stone.

"Wow," Hale shot back. "I resent that."

Like Hale, Stone was never too tired to smile, and had a playful look even now as he pushed hard through the rowing motions. These youngest two members of our pride, Stone at 26 and Hale at 27, were always batting friendly insults back and forth between one another. At 30, I wasn't much older, but I still didn't know where they got their energy from.

Maybe my mind was just occupied with more serious things.

"How much time left?" Stone asked.

"One more minute," I said. "Then we run."

"Thank fuck." Stone pressed on, lifting a hand to push back the bleach-blond sweep of his hair. Needless to say, that bleach-blond was the subject of a lot of Hale's teasing, but nobody could deny that it suited him. As alpha of the pride, I kind of had to appreciate that at least one of us was sporting something like a mane in human form.

It wasn't exactly the most practical haircut for paramilitary operations, but Stone was our medic. I figured I could cut him a little slack.

When the timer finally hit zero, the room gave a collective exhale. All the tension in our muscles faded away to sweat and heat, and there was a fizz of relief in the air as we headed outside.

"Good work today," I said, pausing to pat Preston's shoulder as he passed, and closing the door behind us. "I didn't hear too many complaints. Everybody had good form. Shaping up pretty well for next week."

"If we're not exhausted," said Hale, rolling his shoulders back. "Shit. I wish my lion wasn't so ready to go right now. I want to fall down face-first into a snack."

"You always do," Stone teased. "C'mon. Let's get this over with."

As he reached the edge of the gravel path outside our home, he shifted in the blink of an eye. Where there had once been lithe limbs and tan skin, Stone was now all sand-colored fur — the well-shaped, muscular form of a lion's body, paws pounding against the floor hard enough to leave imprints in the crumbly earth.

The rest of us followed close behind, keeping pace with our medic. Even your average human could probably spot the difference between us, but it was even easier for our pride. Stone's blond hair seemed to be reflected in the lightness of his mane, and how it so closely mirrored the rest of his fur. Flecks of gray were peppered through Preston's dark, near-black mane. Hale stood taller than the rest of us, and with a reddish sheen to him that was absent from his human form. As for me, I was a muddy gray with a mane that lightened at the edges, with muscular limbs that marked me out as leader.

Of course, human eyes wouldn't catch all these details at first glance. For one thing, we were moving quick enough to be easily missed, dust whipping up around us in a storm. After working our human bodies so hard today, this felt like a treat. Like the best kind of cool-down stretch. We wouldn't feel like ourselves if we had no time to do this. Our human forms were fine, but there was something pure and right about this form that we needed every once in a while. However the others experienced it, I could feel the earth pulsing through my paws, connected to me in a way that my other shape wasn't.

We could communicate differently in this form, too. We didn't need to speak to fall into formation, forming a chain that worked perfectly as we made our way through the undergrowth and the tightly-packed forest. We each took turns in the lead, fast and furious as we coursed over gulches and dips in the ground. It was seamless. Nobody had to snarl or roar to advertise their position; we were just aware of each other, as easily as we were aware of ourselves. We barely had to think about it.

This innate sense of flow and cooperation was why we worked so well together as a military unit. Maybe our commanding officer didn't really understand what bonded us so closely. Our shifter status was highly classified information. Still, it was obvious to everyone who came into contact with us how useful our unspoken communication could be in any intense and difficult situation.

This was why we were trusted with such important missions. This was why we were being sent away in ten days. No amount of physical aptitude or training could compare to the kind of team that we had — and our physical skills were top-notch in any case.

It was a tough life. We worked hard, and had little time to ourselves, but the pride kept each other sane and happy. There'd be time for fun and settling down later in our lives.

Probably.

By the time our lion muscles were as exhausted as our human ones, the sun was just about to come down. I took the lead again as we headed back home, feeling the earth cool underneath our paws, and only shifted back again as we reached the yard.

I opened the door, glancing over my shoulder at the sound of Hale's yawn. He had already shifted back, stretching his arms with a slight grimace. "Man. Hard work today. I needed that run."

"I think we all did," I agreed, holding the door open so that each one of them could pass — first Hale, already yawning again, and then Preston and Stone behind him. "But we'll be grateful for being in the best possible shape when we're out there in Sigma territory."

"Damn right."

We flopped into the long angular couch, big enough to hold us all with a little extra space... in human form, at least. Even draped over these soft cushions, ready to be lazy for the rest of the day now, I could see the strength in my pride's arms, and I knew we were ready. I had faith that not only were we likely to succeed in this mission, but we'd do it fast too — and safely.

Still, there was one thing left to discuss before we started our final preparations.

"Guys," I said, glancing over my shoulder. "This place is a dump."

I was only barely exaggerating. As we'd been training so hard, the kitchen had been used to prepare several meals that hadn't quite been cleared away yet, and there were piles of clothes dropped all over the floor from where tired lions had abandoned their human things and never come back for them. Our enhanced shifter senses weren't much of a good thing when you could smell dust in the air, and see crumbs that needed lifting from the carpet all the way across the other side of the room.

This… would not work for our mission.

"We've got time yet to clear it up," said Stone, smoothing the suede of the couch arm all in the same direction. "Really shouldn't take that long."

"Uh-huh," I said. "But we can't have the cabin like this in Sigma."

Preston wrinkled his nose. "Huh. Yeah."

"It's a distraction," I said. "And clearly we've been focusing pretty hard on other things the past week or so. The workload isn't going to be lighter once we're actually out there. Maybe we need to work something out."

"What, like a rota?"

"Hale," said Stone, eyes bright, "we all know you'd never stick to a rota."

"Actually," I pressed on, before Hale could bite back, "I was thinking more like external help. Somebody we'd bring along specifically to take care of the cabin for us."

"A shifter?" said Preston.

I shrugged, considering it. "I don't know. It could be hard to find somebody in time now. It's so last-minute. I think we're going to have to put an ad out in the paper and hope for the best. Maybe go through an agency if we absolutely have to, but… I'd prefer somebody we can approve of ourselves."

"That would be my concern," said Hale, wearing his serious hat for once. "We need somebody trustworthy, and also who understands that the place we're going is not exactly safe. That they need to take any instructions we give them seriously."

"We could interview for that," I agreed, nodding. "Stone? Preston? What do you think?"

"The budget allows for it," confirmed Stone, finally looking up from his cell phone screen. "We have a surplus. I think you're right; I think it makes sense."

"We're going to have to be careful," said Preston. "If they're not a shifter. If they don't know…"

"It wouldn't be the first time we had to keep the secret," Hale pointed out. "We could shift back before we got to the cabin every day."

"Would it be harder to make sure we're not followed, that way?" Preston folded his arms, brow furrowed in concentration as he tried to answer his own question. "I'm not against it. Just want to make sure we're doing the right thing here."

"Let's think about it," I suggested. "We can put out the ad and see who shows up to interview. Trust our instincts. If somebody fits, we'll make it work. If they don't…"

"We teach Hale how to follow a rota," said Stone, dodging as Hale tried to swat his arm.

We had a plan. Now, it just remained to be seen whether it would actually work out for us or not — and if this was really a good idea.

I sipped my coffee as I headed out of Starbucks, even though it was still a little too hot. The barista was so busy it appeared she would run off her feet, but she seemed to like her job a hell of a lot more than I liked mine. I checked my watch, picking up the pace to make sure I reached the station in time to catch the next train home.

I didn't want to spend a single minute more away from home. Today had really taken it out of me.

You would think that sitting behind a desk all day would leave you pretty well-rested, but it was actually the exact opposite. The more time I spent cooped up and staring at expense reports on a computer screen, the more I wanted to run out of that place and never look back — not that I had the energy to run.

The pay was okay. The benefits were reasonable. The commute was long, but it could be a heck of a lot worse.

But didn't I deserve something a little bit more than *okay*?

It felt like I spent most of my life working. A few years ago, I'd left college believing that my life was just about to kick into high gear. Now, I barely saw the friends I'd made there, who I'd felt so close to back then. None of us ever seemed to have time off that coincided. My life had turned into the kind of treadmill I'd only seen in movies and 'before' pictures.

I needed an injection of something good and different. Fast.

Once I finally got a seat on the train and could settle down with my coffee and my evening paper, I fell into the usual routine. I scanned the Missed Connections section first, always hoping in vain that some Prince Charming or other would have seen me across the counter at Subarro and fallen head over heels in love with me. It could happen, right? But for some reason, there were no notices that fit my description today — just like every other day.

Never mind. On to the classified ads.

A couple of people were selling pure-breed puppies. If my apartment allowed pets, I might have considered it, but... not for the thousands of dollars these breeders wanted to charge. Somebody wanted five hundred bucks for an old couch. Judging by the attached picture, it might be worth that if it had four hundred hidden under the seat cushions.

There really wasn't much of interest today. I was about to close the paper and go back to daydreaming with my coffee when my eyes caught on a job advertisement.

Live-in home manager wanted, it read. *Competitive pay. Join our tight-knit team in a remote location for full three-month term, with a near-immediate start. Duties will include cooking, cleaning and general home maintenance. All applicants welcome to inter-view — good personality fit required. Call for details.*

There was nothing special about it. It certainly wasn't my area of work. I studied finance at college, and now I stared at facts and figures all day, preparing detailed cost breakdowns and profit/loss reports. I could cook and clean, of course, but I'd never considered doing it for a living. Not even slightly.

So why was I itching to call that number?

My fingertips hovered over the ad. Could it be that I was just lonely? They mentioned a tight-knit team, which would be a far cry away from the cut-and-dry environment of my office, where nobody exchanged more than a couple of sentences with one another. Either that, or it could be the thought of getting out of the city for a couple of months.

Now that the idea had wormed into my head, I couldn't shake it. The feeling was surreal. I had never even thought about leaving my job before, at least not in a serious way. Now here I was feeling drawn to a random ad in the paper that didn't even cover my expertise. However competitive the pay was, could it really compete with my current salary for my highly-trained job?

I dropped the paper to my lap, frowning down at my coffee. I was probably just tired. I needed to get home, make a quick dinner and binge something on Netflix. If I needed to call that number and set up an interview just to scratch the itch, then so be it. It didn't mean I had to actually *attend* it.

Man, scratch 'make a quick dinner'. I needed takeout tonight. That much was for sure.

When I found myself in an Uber pulling up to a big house outside the city at 5:30pm the following day, I could barely believe I had come this far. Surely I wasn't *really* going to leave my safe, secure office job for this opportunity, no matter how well the interview went? I was probably just setting myself up for an hour of awkwardness and a pointless rejection.

All risk, no reward.

"Alright," said my Uber driver Shanice, giving me a big

cheery grin as she pulled to a stop. "Here you go. Don't look so nervous, okay? You're going to do great."

"Maybe."

"Hey, none of that," she said, wagging a finger at me. "You made a great impression on me. I'm sure they're going to love you. And if you figure out you don't want the job, then… at least you don't have any regrets, you know? You took your shot. That's what life's all about."

"You're adorable," I said, although privately I couldn't help but feel like I needed to stop telling my life story to every friendly stranger I met. Shanice was cool, but she probably didn't want to know about my unnecessary job interview woes. "Thanks for the pep talk. Have a good day!"

I watched the car pull away. I wasn't a nervous person, but I couldn't help chewing the inside of my lip as I walked up to the front door of this house. It looked like a nice place. The advert was asking for a 'good personal fit'. If the people who lived here were really well-off, chances were that I wasn't going to be on their level. I lived paycheck-to-paycheck, pretty much.

Still, I had no choice now. Shanice was already halfway down the street.

I plucked up my courage and rang the doorbell.

When the door opened, I was immediately glad I hadn't run screaming. The guy who opened the door was… well, *really* hot. My first thoughts didn't get any more eloquent than that. I forced my mouth into a smile so that my jaw didn't drop open, and held out my hand,

"Hi," I said, hoping my blush was light and rosy and not completely humiliating. "I'm Jess Dorsey. I'm supposed to be here for an interview, though I think I'm a little early."

"Don't worry about that," he said. When he took my hand, I felt his grip strong and serious around mine. His hand was huge, and his jaw so firm and square that it looked like somebody had cut it that way on purpose. "It's great that you're here. Come on through. And, uh. Sorry about the mess. I swear it's not usually this bad."

"Hey, no problem. That's what you're advertising for, right?"

"I think this is beyond the scope of one person's daily duties," he said, throwing me a sheepish look over his shoulder. God, he had a handsome smile. "We've just been a little busy getting ready for our trip, that's all. It's kind of mounted up. I'm Hale, by the way."

We stepped into a living room space, with a huge corner couch and huge bay windows. Of course, the room wasn't really what I paid attention to — because as well as Hale, there were three other intimidatingly good-looking men scattered around the place.

*Holy shit. What do they **do**...?*

"Alright," said Hale, clapping his hands together. "Jessica. Like I said, I'm Hale. This is Preston, with the piercings. Stone's the bottle blonde."

Stone threw him a withering look and shook his head at me. "The shit I get from this guy," he said. "You wouldn't believe."

"And I'm Blake."

My eyes shifted away from Stone's easygoing smile to a much more serious face. His deep grey eyes seemed to carry a lot of weight, and his dark, short-shaven hair had a pretty military aesthetic. All this, and he also had muscular arms even thicker than the rest of his colleagues. He looked almost dangerous. The kind of guy you'd like to have on your side, and definitely wouldn't want as an opponent.

"We appreciate you coming down here on such short notice," said Blake, gesturing at an armchair that sat beside the couch. I dropped down into it, trying not to look nervous or outnumbered — though of course, I definitely was outnumbered. "We know it's a fast turnaround. We really should have started looking a long time ago, but… as you can see, we haven't been fully organized for a little while."

I smiled, appraising the room around me. It was a little messy, sure, but nothing too heinous. I didn't feel uncomfortable, or felt like I'd need to take a shower as soon as I stepped outside. "It's not so bad," I insisted. "Hale was telling me that you've been pretty busy getting ready for these three months away."

Blake nodded. "That's right. And we'd like to tell you more about that, but… before we do, I just want to point out that what we do is pretty serious work. It's classified, and we'll need you to sign non-disclosure forms and complete background checks if you're successful."

"Don't worry about all that," Stone advised. "It's just government rules. If we trust you, we trust you. We like to think we're pretty good judges of character."

I nodded, taking it all in. "I understand. It's fine with me, anyway. I've got nothing to hide."

"Open book, huh?" said Stone.

I smiled, spreading my hands. "What can I say?"

Casual as I was acting, this was all very strange. Government rules. Classified. Maybe the 'military' feel I had detected on Blake wasn't far off the mark. What exactly had I walked into?

"You wouldn't be doing anything dangerous yourself, of course," Blake continued. "What we described in the ad is exactly what we're looking for. While we focus on the reason we're out there, you'll be helping us by keeping everything running smoothly in a domestic sense."

"Right," I agreed. "Making sure there's food on the table and clean clothes to wear."

"Honestly, we're not real fussy," Hale added. "We're not going to expect shiny sinks and three-course dinners. Probably, we'll be able to take care of a lot of things ourselves. We just want to make sure we've got you there to handle the basics if we're pulling really long hours."

"I get you," I said. "That makes sense."

My eyes flicked over the four men again. Stone seemed the least scary, but he was still the kind of model-pretty you'd follow right away on Instagram. The one with the fleck of premature grey in his hair and the ear piercings — Preston? — hadn't spoken at all, but he was definitely paying attention. I felt he was observing me, not in a creepy way, but it still made me a little hot under the collar. I hoped those blue eyes found that I was up to par.

"We're leaving in one week exactly now," said Blake. He spared a glance at each of his colleagues, then turned back to me. "Since the location is classified, you'll need to travel with us, and we really would need you to stay for the full three months. Could even be longer, depending on how things go for us. Will that be okay with you?"

I nodded, listening. Then I realized something.

"Oh. Does that mean I got the job...?"

My cheeks flushed. That was quite an assumption to make, but something in the tone of his voice sounded like he was making an offer — not checking, just in case. I looked at each of the team members again, hoping I hadn't made a fool of myself.

"If our terms work for you, and you're still interested," said Blake, with a little smile. "Then yes. We'd love to have you join the team."

I flushed. They hadn't even discussed it. How could they possibly know that I was the right person for the job? But despite the fact that this didn't make sense, I couldn't fight the happy feeling that was flooding through my chest. As certain as I had been only twenty minutes ago that this was a pointless endeavor, I was thrilled. In fact, I was already composing my letter of resignation. Hopefully one week's notice would be enough.

If not, well… tough.

"I'd be happy to," I said despite myself, feeling the hair on the backs of my arms stand up. This was sheer madness, but at the same time, it felt so *right*. "Thank you so much. I'll start making my preparations right away."

My Uber driver on the way home wasn't nearly as talkative. It was then that I realized I hadn't even asked about the pay. No wonder they offered me the job on the spot. They probably thought I was the dumbest candidate they'd seen — but even so, I still couldn't bring myself to regret accepting their offer. Something felt *good* about that group of men, even beyond how painfully attractive they were. I couldn't quite put my finger on it yet, but… hey.

I was about to have three whole months to work it out.

HALE

The drive to the cabin was long and uneventful, but it gave us an excellent opportunity to confirm that we were 100% right about Jessica. No matter who was driving and who was hanging out with her in the back of the van, she seemed totally comfortable with us. It was obvious that she was a little nervous, but that made sense. She had no idea where she was going, and had only met us a couple of times.

Still, she was managing to laugh and joke along with us. We heard a little about her family, and how lame her past job was. The story about her asshole boss' reaction to her leaving with such short notice had us all in stitches.

All our instincts about her had been right. When we met each other's eyes in that brief moment before Blake offered her the job just one week ago, we had already been pretty sure. Now, finally pulling up to the cabin after many hours of driving, there could be absolutely no uncertainty left. At least, not on our part.

We probably still had to earn her full trust.

"Alright," I said, closing the door behind her as she

climbed out of the van. "Honey, we're home." Was it weird that I was so drawn to hang around her? Probably not. She was a beautiful woman. Her smile was really charming. Even when it had been my turn to drive, I could see her lighting up the van every time she flashed it.

I wasn't the kind of guy to get smitten, but... suffice to say, I knew she had my attention.

"Shall I get my bag?"

"Not yet," said Blake, heading straight for the front door. "We'll get them later. Let's just go settle in first. I think we've earned that."

The cabin itself was pretty basic, with wood-panel walls and an open fire. The place was open-plan on the inside, and not quite as spacious as our home, but it would definitely do for the time we spent here. Most of the time, we'd be working in shifts anyhow; we wouldn't need to share the space altogether much.

"Hale," said Blake, nodding down the hallway. "Why don't you show Jessica to her room?"

"You know, Jess is fine," she said, following after me with an awkward smile. "But I'd love to see home for the next few months, sure."

I swept my arm, leading her down the corridor. There was only one direction to go, so it wasn't exactly a grand tour, but there was no harm in playing. I opened the door for her with a slight bow. "Right this way, madam."

"You're too kind, sir," she said, bowing right back. She stepped into the room and took a look around. Judging by the smile on her face, she wasn't disappointed. "It's nice. Much bigger than my bedroom back in the city."

"I guess that's the benefit of being out here in the wilderness," I said, choosing not to tell her that we'd given her the biggest room on purpose. She seemed like the type to try and refuse it. "No Starbucks unless you drive for two hours, but… man, plenty of room to swing a cat."

"I will not be swinging any cats," she said, dropping her bag onto the bed with a playful smile. "But it'll be nice to go through my morning yoga routine without bumping my head on the dresser, for one thing."

"Right, right," I said, folding my arms. "I thought the same thing."

Jess smiled at me, shaking her head. "Don't make fun of me. We can't be all that bendy with muscles like that."

"Glad you've noticed." I grinned, pleased by the blush on her face. "You want to see the rest of the place, anyway? May as well get familiar."

Back out onto the main corridor, I pointed out the rooms on the side opposite to hers. "Alright. That door's Blake and Stone's room. This one is mine and Preston's. Bathroom on the end there will probably be ours, since you, Blake and Stone are all en-suite, but… you know. We're easy."

"And this is the main room," she said stepping out into it. "Kitchen, dining room and living room all in one."

"Right you are," I said. "Pretty cozy, I guess. Convenient."

"Does that door lead to a garden?"

She stepped over to it, peering out through the glass. I pulled up beside her. "It does," I said, "but you might want to watch how often you're out alone, especially after dark. Not to freak you out, but… you know. Safety first, on a job like this."

"Oh." She blinked, glancing at me. "You aren't kidding…?"

"No, ma'am." I ruffled my hair, teasing my fingers through the longer bits on top. I kept my voice serious to make sure she could tell the difference; it was easy to forget that strangers couldn't immediately detect when I was and wasn't joking. "I mean… don't be scared, you know? We wouldn't have you here if it was unsafe. You want to go out and get some fresh air, you're more than welcome. I just wouldn't stray too far, just in case."

"Got it."

I could see I'd unnerved her. It made me feel bad, but even stronger than that it made me want to make her feel safe again. It'd probably be weird to put my arm around her this early on, wouldn't it? Instead I shifted between my feet, opening the door to take a few steps outside. Hopefully that would prove the situation wasn't too dire. "Nice out here, actually. Looks like somebody had a vegetable garden here once."

"Shame we don't have time to restart it," she said. "Bet you guys would love eating fresh."

"Oh, 'cos of this?" I tapped my bicep, wrinkling my nose. "Nah. That's all Taco Bell."

"Jessica, your bag is in your room," Blake called. "Just in case you want it."

"Thank you!" she called back. "And honestly, really — Jess is fine…"

I watched her go, fighting the instinct to let my eyes drift down to her ass. *Maybe* something could happen between us further down the line, but I really didn't want to push it. She seemed like a cool person in general, and we had three whole months to spend here. I didn't want to make things awkward or uncomfortable for her, or for anybody else on the team.

But she'd definitely noticed my arms…

JESSICA

This whole endeavor was still definitely the biggest risk I'd ever taken in my professional life, but I felt more certain about it as time went by. The drive to the cabin was long, but it gave me a chance to get to know my new employers — or colleagues, really. They treated me more like an equal than as a subordinate, and I appreciated that.

Blake seemed pretty insistent on calling me by my full name, but I hoped to be able to persuade him out of that before long.

The first day after we arrived, things were pretty calm. The boys still had some unpacking to do, and I got up early to get breakfast going. The smell of cooking bacon soon tempted four hungry Norths out of their rooms, just in time to have it served up fresh and crackling onto their plates.

"I knew this was a good idea," said Hale, ruffling a bit of life into his hair. "I think you just earned every cent we're going to pay you with this one meal."

"You haven't eaten it yet," I warned. "You remember my training is in finance, right?"

"The culinary courses missed out," said Stone, already

20

halfway through his plate. "You're amazing. Thank you for this."

"You're welcome, Mr. North. That's why I'm here!" As they carried on digging in, I remembered another question I had. It was a slightly awkward one, so I figured it was better to get it out of the way early. "Hey, uh… listen. I have to ask. You're all Norths. So, are you… brothers…?"

They certainly didn't look like it.

Stone and Hale glanced at one another, and Blake sat up a little straighter to answer my question. "It's a long story," he said, "but no, we're not technically related. We consider each other family, but we're not connected up that way."

I nodded, but that hadn't really clarified things.

"More like cousins," said Stone, trying to be helpful. "Think of it that way. We grew up together. Our families are so close they're basically all the same thing."

That didn't explain the shared surname, but I decided to give up on asking before things got even more awkward. "I see. And now you all work together."

"We make a good team," said Hale. "The kind of work we do, you need to be able to communicate quick and fast. You need to be able to trust each other. Just kind of makes sense."

"Plus," said Stone, "we each have different skills that complement each other. I've studied a lot of first-response medicine, so I'm our unofficial medic."

"Weapons and communication," said Preston, holding up a hand. It was one of the only times he'd spoken directly to me so far, and it surprised me to see him meeting my eyes. I'd already decided that he was deathly shy — either that, or he didn't like me.

Blake pushed his plate away from himself, finally finished. "I take the lead."

"And I back him up," said Hale. "Blake's a pretty strategic

thinker. Very methodical. Great ideas. I'm more of a people person."

I looked at each of them, impressed by the wide array of skills. I still didn't really know what they were here for, but I'd heard 'military' and 'classified'. I'd signed a non-disclosure agreement — and now the word 'weapons' had been thrown into the mix. They were so capable that I felt a little intimidated simply to be in their presence. Trying to make light of that, I held up my hands. "And I… make a mean breakfast."

"Let's not undervalue that," said Stone. "I'd take breakfast over Hale's supposed people skills any day."

"You see what I put up with?" said Hale. "Every day!"

"Not every day," said Blake. "Because this is the part of the conversation where I remind you that *I* am working with Stone on shift this time, and you'll be teamed up with Preston."

"You're not all working together?" I asked, then pulled a face and covered my mouth. "Sorry. It's none of my business."

"It's fine," Blake insisted. "It's like Hale told you before. The fact that you're here at all proves that we trust you. If we need to keep something from you, we'll let you know; otherwise, ask away."

His eyes were so intense that I couldn't help but blush and avert my gaze. "Okay," I said. "I'll bear that in mind. Thank you."

"No," Blake continued. "You're right. We're not all working together. To make sure we're covering as much ground as possible in these initial stages, we'll be operating in shifts. We won't be sleeping or eating at the same time so that there's somebody out working almost at all times."

That's intense. What are they really working on here?

"That doesn't mean you need to make every meal twice,"

Stone added. "We can reheat stuff. We're not trying to work you twice as hard as we agreed."

"You're not eating reheated food if I can help it," I insisted. Now that we actually *had* discussed pay, I knew that I was going to be compensated for every single hour I spent here, even while asleep. There was no way I was going to slack off on those terms. "You're going to be working so hard; I'm sure you'll be exhausted. The least I can do is make sure you have something good to eat when you get back."

"Just don't feel pressured," said Stone. "That's all we ask."

As it turned out, however, I didn't think I could feel pressured if I tried. As the boys began working in shifts, we started to settle into a routine. Even with two sets of meals to prepare, I didn't have much work to do. It felt like the greatest part of my day was spent relaxing, with very little to occupy my time except reading and messing around with the hand-weights that the Norths had brought to the cabin with them.

If the off-shift men were awake, we could spend a little time talking and hanging out. The more time I got with them, the more I grew to like their company. Before long, I knew I'd be hoping to spend even more time together. I just hoped that sometime soon, we'd get to a point where I didn't feel butterflies in my stomach every time one of them made direct eye contact with me. 'Cos this, right now, with all the blushing? This wasn't me at all.

STONE

The first few weeks of the mission went by without any incident. It was easy to forget that we were here to hunt down an extremist sleeper cell that the government had identified as a national security threat. So far, we had seen neither head nor tail of their gun-toting selves — and every time we came in out of the cold, we either had a hot meal waiting for us, or just about to be served.

Even better than the meal was the company. Jess was already proving to be exactly the kind of company we needed. She had a great sense of humor, even if it veered a little too self-deprecating for my liking. She seemed to feel inadequate around us sometimes, as though we were some kind of superhero force and she was just our backup. I hoped she'd soon realize that we were just a bunch of goofballs who happened to have some pretty useful skills.

Well. A bunch of goofballs and Blake.

I loved the leader of our pride just like the others, but he had such a serious outlook that I couldn't accurately call him a goofball. He seemed to carry the weight of the world on his shoulders, and I often wondered whether he got enough sleep at night. Even now, as he could hear Jess asking us a question, his eyes were so intense and serious that I figured something else must be on his mind — right up until the moment he answered her.

"It's because Hale is my second in command," Blake explained; she had asked, maybe just to make polite conversation, why we always went out in the same pairs. "We have to keep separate in case something should happen to one of us."

"You're in that much danger?" she asked.

I gave Blake a look, hoping that he wouldn't alarm her. Luckily, he seemed to be thinking along the same lines. "It's mostly a precaution," he said, pouring himself another glass of water from the pitcher. "A military habit, I guess. They're hard to kick."

"Are you all military-trained?"

He nodded, but as he'd just taken a mouthful of water, I stepped up to answer.

"We are now. When the team was formed, Blake, Hale and Preston were all Marines. I wasn't. I'd just been working on my medical studies, and I had to go through basic training before I could officially be considered a part of this. 'Course, we already worked together as a team pretty well, since we'd grown up together, but… training made it official."

"Wow," she said. "All pretty hardcore, huh?"

"I'm going to assume you're not teasing me," I said. "For your own safety. That's how hardcore I am." I grinned at her laughter, turning to follow her progress around the table as she carried her own plate to eat with us. "Laughing to stave off the fear," I said. "I see how it is."

"I'll make sure I don't turn my back on you," she said.

"That's right."

Blake glanced up from his maps, giving both of us a crooked smile. "The day Stone keeps his mouth shut for long enough to sneak up on anyone with their back turned, I'll be shocked."

"Hey," I said, pretending to be wounded. "I'm not Hale."

"You're the next best thing, while he's out," Blake insisted. "Or next worst, I guess."

"So, as I was saying," I said, turning to Jess. "We work *very* well together."

Our eyes met. She gave me a wicked smile, chin propped up on her hand. The blonde hair she hadn't gathered into a loose bun was falling into her eyes — and so was I. Maybe I was imagining things, but it felt like she felt closer to me than any of the others. That kind of made sense. I was the youngest, and acted like it; of the four North men, I was probably least intimidating to an outsider. Besides, Blake teasing me about being a mini-Hale wasn't far off the mark. I was pretty good with people too and liked to think I'd done a good job of making Jess feel at home here in the cabin.

Whether that would lead to more, I wasn't sure — but I had gained a friend I liked very much either way. It just remained to be seen whether I'd be pining over her in secret.

Well, it probably wouldn't be a secret for very long. Hale would pick up on it the second he sees us together. For as much as we messed with each other, he was my best friend, and the other two members of the pride weren't far behind. They'd be able to see my attraction to Jess written all over my face. I could only hope that she wouldn't be able to read me so easily — or that if she could, she liked what she saw.

"Alright," said Blake, folding up his maps. "I'm going to hit the shower, and then hit the hay. It's going to be a long day tomorrow."

"Okay, boss. See you in the morning."

"Night, Blake!" said Jess, waving him off.

And with that, it was just us. I felt even more drawn to her now that we were alone, but I knew it wasn't right to push it. I didn't even want to. We had plenty of time to get to know each other better at our own pace — even if she made my stomach flip when she looked at me.

"Well," she said. "I better get started on these dishes."

"I can handle those. You cooked."

"Absolutely not," said Jess, snatching my plate away before I could carry it up to the sink. "This is what you're paying me for, and it's about all I can do for you."

I pressed my hands together, giving her a sheepish smile. "Doesn't feel right to sit here and watch you, though. You've got to at least let me help."

"You're providing company," she said. "That's how you can help. If you just- ah!"

My ears pricked at the sharp intake of breath, and I stood from the table to go to her immediately. She lifted her hands out of the sink, her left hand gripping her right. There was a nasty cut in her palm.

"Whoa," I said. "What happened?"

"Sharp knife in the water," she said, through gritted teeth. "Must've landed upright when I dropped it in the bowl."

I reached across to drain the sink. Sure enough, a small, sharp cutting knife stood upright, wedged between a bowl and a pan.

"Clearly, I'm an idiot," she said.

"No, no. Could've happened to anyone. You keep hold of your hand, okay? I'll be back in a beat."

"I can manage," she called after me. "Honestly, I don't need any fuss."

"Listen," I said, returning with my basic first aid kit. "I'm the medic, and the last time this team saw bloodshed it was because Preston got a paper-cut. Let me be useful."

I was half-teasing, but the wound in her hand did actually look pretty nasty. If untreated, it could easily get infected —

and it was definitely going to hurt tomorrow, especially if I didn't bandage it up correctly.

"Here," I said, guiding her to the table. "Come sit down. I'll clean and wrap it."

"Do I have to?"

"And here I was thinking you'd be a model patient," I said, taking a seat beside her. I opened the kit and dabbed a little cleaning solution onto a cotton pad. "Fair warning. This is going to sting a little."

"I can take it."

She winced as I applied the solution, dabbing it carefully around the wounded area. There was a lot of blood, but thankfully the cut wasn't as deep as it looked. The blade had gone into her hand at an angle, and thankfully missed anything that could have caused real damage — her tendons or her muscles, for example.

"Almost done," I said, giving it one last wipe. "Alright. Sorry about that."

"You'll notice I didn't complain," she said. "I'm a big girl."

"I did notice. You could've been forgiven for cursing like a sailor," I said, laying some gauze over the cut. "I know what that stuff feels like."

"Maybe you're just a big baby."

I grinned at her. "Probably, yeah." Though she smiled back at me, I could see that a little color had faded out of her cheeks. Jess was strong, but clearly it hurt more than she was willing to show. I made sure to keep my touch gentle as I bandaged her up.

"There we go. My medic skills aren't a waste after all."

A few moments later, I realized that I hadn't let go of her hand. Nor had she pulled it away. Not thinking, I traced my thumb gently over the top of the bandage. Had it been skin to skin, it'd have been a feather-light touch — probably ticklish.

She swallowed, and the color returned to her cheeks.

God, was she ever beautiful!

I let go of her hand, fighting off the urge to lean closer and kiss her. This was too much, too fast. I didn't want to overwhelm her or make things awkward for the rest of her time here. I scratched the back of my neck, smiling down at the table.

"Anyway, you're welcome. And now you're going to *have* to let me take care of the dishes."

"Oh, come on!"

I gave a big exaggerated shrug and stood up from the table, picking up the rest of the plates. "For all I know, this was your plan all along. I'm onto you, Dorsey."

"Yeah, yeah," she said. She was looking at her hand. I made my way to the sink. When I looked back at her, I could see that the back of her neck and the tips of her ears were all a bright, bashful pink.

I could still feel Stone's touch on my hand, both under and around the bandage. It was more pronounced than the pain — the dancing, electric tingles that reminded me exactly where our skin had come into contact. My heart was pounding, and I couldn't help but feel self-conscious as I said my goodnight and headed to my own room.

Had he noticed, I wondered, what effect he had on me?

As I settled into bed for the night, setting my alarm ready to wake up and make breakfast, I could still feel my heart going at hummingbird pace in my chest. I couldn't settle down. Was it normal to feel this way about somebody you'd only just met? I'd never been a head-over-heels kind of girl. Even worse, I had to be honest with myself.

It wasn't just Stone that set my pulse racing.

Blake's 'oh-so-serious' persona sometimes cracked into a soft smile, and I could feel myself melting every time I saw it. Preston still didn't speak much, but there was something intriguing and appealing in his dark eyes. Hale was so charming that it intimidated me, and I could feel my tongue tying up around him.

It was frustrating. Here I was, a fully grown woman, and I was acting like a flustered teenager over these four men. I could barely settle down to rest without thinking about the way Stone had looked at me. It felt like he was about to kiss me.

Whether it was true or not, I couldn't get the thought out of my head. I imagined him just on the other side of the wall beside my bed, and swallowed hard.

If I didn't ignore the heat beginning to pool between my legs, things were quickly going to get out of hand.

In the morning, when I finally dragged myself out of bed, I didn't feel a whole lot different. As I heard Stone getting his morning shower and head out to greet Blake, I realized in a jolt that they'd be leaving within the hour. Sure, Preston and Hale would be coming back — but for the better part of the day, there would *always* be at least two of them out there in danger, trying to complete their mysterious government task.

I couldn't help but feel afraid for them. Of course, they were more than capable of looking after themselves, but I was attached to them now. I couldn't imagine how I'd feel if anything should happen to any one of them.

"You know where you're going out there, don't you, Blake?"

"Hm?" He looked up from his maps, jolted out of a train of thought. "Sorry, Jessica. Jess."

"I just don't want you all to get lost, or stumble into some trouble, or… anything like that."

Blake smiled, folding his hands together. There it was —

that rare flash of softness. "We'll be fine; this is not our first rodeo. You don't need to worry about us."

"If you say so."

He nodded to my hand. "Stone was telling me about your hand. Maybe it's us who should be worrying about you...?"

"I swear I'm not completely incompetent," I insisted, hiding the wounded hand with the other one. "It was hidden in the water, and I feel really stupid about it, and-"

"I'm only teasing you," said Blake. Now that he said that, I could see the lightness in his eyes. Maybe he wasn't all seriousness after all. It would just take a little time for me to learn how to read his body language. "How does it feel this morning?"

"It's not so bad," I lied, flexing my fingers. "I'm just going to have to give up on the hand-weights for a few days, I think."

"That's probably for the best," he agreed. At that, a damp-haired Stone walked into the room, a towel flung over his shoulder. I felt my ears burn red and rushed to the counter to bring his breakfast over.

"Hey, morning, Stone," Blake continued. "I was just looking at the route. Considering the good visibility today, I was thinking of diverting us to make sure we're not left too open across the valley..."

I felt grateful for the excuse to be silent, giving them the space to discuss more important plans. This wasn't like me, but I didn't trust myself to have an eloquent conversation with Stone right now. The dreams I'd had last night were one thing. Having to see him look like that in person was quite another — and it didn't help that Blake was equally easy on the eyes.

My life had taken a strange turn over the past few weeks. I could never have seen myself taking this job just a month ago. I certainly couldn't have guessed I'd be spending my time ducking away from making eye contact with *really* attractive men.

Not least because it was usually in my nature to catch that eye contact and wink.

I caught a few words of their conversation, even as I tried to block it out. They were words you couldn't help but hear. *Explosives. Radicalized.* I shuddered, even with my hands under the warm water of the kitchen sink. We all heard those words way too often on news channels today, and now here we were in the midst of some operation or other that faced it down directly. I was more than likely safe in here, but the North boys would be staring it down every single day.

"Jess...?"

I jumped, looking back over my shoulder. "Hi. Sorry."

"It's okay," said Stone, giving me a particularly stomach-melting lopsided grin. "Just... wasn't sure you should be soaking your hands too much. Gotta keep that bandage on nice and tight until your hand's had a chance to heal, right?"

"Right," I said, shaking the water off my hands. "Yes."

He paused, folding his arms. "So. You're just going to go straight back to doing that as soon as we leave, aren't you?"

"No," I lied. Badly.

"I'll take it with me," he warned. "And when that excess weight leads to the failure of the entire mission, this one-" he pointed at Blake, "will be real mad at you."

I managed a smile, leaning back against the counter. This was the really difficult thing about Stone. He was gorgeous, but he was also so easy to get along with. He didn't make my stomach flip with intimidation like Blake did.

He just... made it flip another way.

"Fine," I said. "I'll leave it. I promise. But I hasten to remind you that this is the whole reason I'm here."

"Can't hurt to leave it for 24 hours," said Blake, standing

up from the table. His smile was fainter, but just as sincere. "Alright. Thanks for breakfast."

Stone was already wolfing down his food, so I took a few steps after Blake instead, feeling compelled by force to ask the question bubbling up inside me. I knew it was stupid. Still, I couldn't help but say it.

"Blake…? You guys will be careful out there, right?"

His smile softened a fraction, glancing over my shoulder at Stone and then back to me again. "We'll be fine," he said. "Careful might not be the right word for this job, but we know when to take the risk and when to pull back. I can promise you that."

I nodded, suddenly embarrassed. He didn't seem to think I was an idiot as he nodded back and walked away, but I felt like one.

After all, what kind of domestic assistant cared so much about her employers after mere days that she *needed* to ask them to take care of themselves outside, as if they weren't professionals? As if they hadn't done this before a thousand times, without me there to warn them?

*I*n truth, I started feeling under the weather after the first couple of days at the cabin. I kept it to myself at first. Most of the time, these kind of head colds just disappeared on their own, and I knew how important this operation was. To duck out because I felt a little stuffed up would be useless cowardice.

When I woke up on the eighth day, however, it was a different story entirely.

My entire head was spinning. I couldn't stand up from the bed without losing my balance a little, and I knew for damn sure I couldn't close one eye and stay upright — let alone look through a sight on a weapon. I'd be no use to Hale like this, or to anyone.

I wasn't planning on taking time out. I figured Stone would have something to patch me up with. Unfortunately, my partner had other ideas. Hale took one look at me and steered me back to bed by the shoulders.

"Nope," he said. "No way. Sleep."

"You can't go out by yourself."

"I'll recon for Blake and Stone on their shift. Don't worry

about what I'm going to do. You just… get your head back down onto the pillow. You look like death."

To tell the truth, I felt like it. To some degree, I was grateful to sink back down into the sheets — but before I fell asleep again, the dominant emotion was guilt. I wasn't here to lie down and languish in the cabin. I was here to perform a task for our government, and in support of the rest of my pack. I was here to keep my country safe. I was…

I was asleep again within minutes.

When I opened my eyes again, the room wasn't spinning so badly around me, but I was still disoriented. I had no conception of what time it was. With Hale's bed empty beside me and the border of light around the curtains fairly dim, I could only assume that he, Blake and Stone were still out working. The cabin was quiet enough.

I slipped my feet out of bed, but soon realized I wasn't healthy enough to stand. The exertion of trying had me enveloped in a coughing fit.

"Preston…?"

I shrank a little as the petite, blonde form of Jessica Dorsey stepped in through the doorway. Her smile was soft and apologetic. "Sorry to barge in," she said. "I don't want to invade your privacy. Just… that's a hell of a cough, you know? Had to make sure you weren't dying."

"Not dying," I clarified, throat still raspy. "Just sick."

"Uh huh. Hale said you weren't doing too good," she said, leaning against the wall slightly. I hadn't spent much time with her yet, as much as I loved to hear her talk to the others. She was so bright and bubbly, and I didn't feel like my quiet sarcasm quite measured up.

Okay, maybe I was a little shy.

"Here," she said, ducking back out again. "This is silly of me. Let me get you some water."

"I'm fine," I insisted, but she had already disappeared.

When she returned only a minute or so later, it wasn't just water in her hands. She was holding a tray, complete with a couple of slices of toast and a chopped-up red apple. "You didn't have to do that."

"And you don't have to eat it," she insisted. "Not if you don't feel like it. I just wanted you to have something, just in case. Sorry, the toast might be a little cold now. I *did* keep it under a little heat, but…"

"It's perfect," I assured her, already trying to sit up a little more in bed. Whatever Jess said, leaving this food uneaten was not an option. She'd gone to the trouble of making it for me, so I'd try to eat it. End of story. "This is sweet of you. Thank you. Please don't feel like you have to play nurse."

"Please," she said. "I'm always the mom friend anyway."

She hovered at the doorway. From the crooked twist in the corner of her smile, I began to realize that I wasn't the only one who was shy. Knowing that made things a little easier, somehow.

"You don't strike me as the mom friend," I countered, leaning forward to adjust the pillow behind me. As I struggled, Jess crossed the room to take it out of my hands. "Okay, I take that back. Yes, you do."

"You're welcome," she said, with playful sarcasm. This close to me, I could smell her perfume — light enough not to make my dizzy head feel worse, but still distinctively fresh and floral. She was summer personified, especially when she smiled. Like now. "I'm sorry," she said. "Here I am telling you I don't want to hijack your privacy, and now I'm fluffing up your pillows. I can't help myself."

"It's okay," I said. "Don't be sorry."

"I actually kind of figured I scared you," she said. The shyness tugged her gaze out of mine, but she managed to pick it back up. When our eyes met again, I saw a flutter of attraction that took me aback. So far, I'd figured she had a crush on Stone.

Maybe I was wrong.

"I wasn't trying to be unfriendly," I said. "I hope it didn't come across like that. And you don't scare me, either. You're great. I'm just... kind of quiet, I guess."

"The strong, silent type," Jess said. "I know it."

She took a few steps back to sit in the armchair. I felt my whole body relax at the thought that she wouldn't be leaving any time soon, and it took my breath away as much as the coughing fit had. I'd spoken to her so little so far that it had escaped notice, but... the way I felt in her company, particularly under the heat of her sole attention, was overpowering.

"Well, Preston," she said, folding her hands. "Now you're a captive patient, no more strong-and-silencing. I want to get to know you while I have the chance."

It was much easier to ignore the lights on my vision and the room swaying around me with her pretty face to focus on. I shrugged, turning one of the rings in my ear and trying to play it cool.

"Sure," I said. "What do you want to know?"

It would be a lie to say I wanted Preston to stay sick. Obviously, I wanted him feeling at his best — but by the same token, I couldn't honestly say I regretted his illness either. He seemed to be less uncomfortable every day, and in the interim I had plenty of time to spend one-on-one with him, learning his unique and playful sense of humor without the hustle and bustle of his three brothers-at-arms to distract me.

Blake and Hale's handsomeness still intimidated me, and I could barely take my mind off Stone. Now I just happened to have another North man making me blush too, and this one was at home 24 hours a day.

It didn't help that I seemed to make him shy too. The tips of his ears lit up red whenever I came into the room, and it put a crooked smile on his face that I couldn't stop thinking about. As he started healing up and feeling a little better, it wasn't far from my mind that we could be so much more than colleagues if one of us just made the first move.

It was four days later that I heard his bedroom door creak open behind me. I was standing at the hob, getting some bacon ready for his lunch, and when I turned around to check on the sound, I was pleasantly surprised to see him emerging from the room.

"Hey," I said, beaming. "You're up and out."

"At last," he agreed. "The cabin isn't spinning around me. I feel pretty clear-headed, actually. Seems like I turned a corner."

"Good! That's what I like to hear."

We shared a smile. I had to duck my head under the pretense of focusing on the bacon; I could feel my heart lifting in my chest.

"I'm gonna grab a shower while I still can," he said eventually. I could still hear the smile in his voice. "Then, uh… that bacon smells *really* good."

"It's all yours," I promised. "You get yourself clean. I'll be ready to fill you up when you get back."

The sound of the shower switching on had my heart racing. I was already flushed in the warmth of the kitchen, but now I was heating up in an entirely different way. An image of him standing under the stream of water, his pale, bare skin slippery with soap, hung around vivid and relentless in my head. I swallowed, giving up on shutting it out. Maybe if I embraced the thought, it would go away of its own accord.

I could hear blood rushing in my ears. This intensity of feeling was so unlike me that I was almost concerned. The last time I'd fallen so head over heels for anybody, I'd been a teenager. Now here I was feeling pulled towards Preston like I'd been drugged — only it didn't feel like a bad thing. I wasn't unwilling. Quite the opposite. It felt like I was coaxing myself into a state of desperate hunger.

How long had I been single? What had it done to me?

And when had the shower stopped running?

I leaned against the counter with both hands, blinking

down at the wooden surface. My heart was pounding hard enough that I could see the shifting fabric of my shirt fluttering. In a minute or two he'd be coming back into the room, and I needed to get a hold on myself.

"Jess...?"

Too late. I turned to face him, trying to pull on a mask of normalcy. If it worked, I'd be surprised. I could feel my eyes raking over his handsome face, reading the concern on his features. Watching a bead of water drip from his pushed-back hair over the angular lines of his face. Seeing the way the light caught his premature silver streak.

Was I sick, I wondered? Was this how he had felt, days ago? I didn't feel dizzy, but I didn't feel like myself either. As he crossed the room towards me, eyes darkening as the concern left and something else, much deeper and more confident, replaced it.

"I just... I had this idea that you needed me," he said, voice low and sincere. "I can't explain it. I couldn't get the thought out of my head."

It was like he was explaining it to himself as much as to me. Maybe he felt the same strange pull that I did. Maybe it had just been *way* too long since I'd gotten laid.

He swallowed, and I watched the bob of his throat as he took another few prowling steps closer to me — then his tongue, darting out to wet his lips. Back against the counter, I tilted back my neck to look up at him as he approached. He was so tall. Even as he reached me and I smoothed my hands up over his arms, I had to stand on my tiptoes to wrap my arms around his neck.

"I'm sorry," he said. "I don't want to push you. But there's just... something about you."

"You're not pushing me."

"No?" he said. His eyes were so careful and serious. "You want it?"

"I want it. Want you. Yes."

A wave of relief hit both of us at once. He leaned down to close the gap between us, pressing his lips down against mine. I wasn't sure how things had escalated so quickly, but now that they had I had no complaints. No regrets. I tangled my hands into the still-damp hair on the back of his head, moaning quietly against his lips at the pressure of his hips against mine. Already, I could feel how rock-hard he was against me; his hands scored a fire-hot line over the shape of my hips, down towards my thighs.

"You're so beautiful."

I groaned, head tipping back as his hands caressed back up my side. "Don't."

"You are," he insisted, leaning down to press a line of not-so-gentle kisses on my neck. "Is it wrong to tell you I can't stop thinking about you? All the time, ever since we got here. Right from the start."

I felt like I was falling, even pinned between his firm body and the wooden curve of the counter at my back. My heart-beat was picking up by the seconds. "No," I said, tipping my head back for his access. "It isn't wrong. I — yeah. Me too…"

It wasn't a lie. I just thought it best not to tell him that I'd felt similar things for all the North boys, in different ways. At different times.

I closed my eyes, feeling him take my weight.

"Shall I take you somewhere else?"

"God. Yes."

My legs fastened tight around him. I could feel his heart pounding against mine, our chests pressed close together as he lifted me through the kitchen and to the doorway of the room he shared with Hale. As he laid me down on the bed and stepped back to pull off his shirt, I took one moment to drink in how surreal this was — as though a naughty dream had come to life.

Judging by the bulge in his briefs as he tugged his jeans down, this would be a very naughty dream indeed.

I pulled my shirt over my head, hair already a little messy in my ponytail. I wished I had worn more exciting under-wear today, but Preston didn't seem to mind. His eyes dark-ened as he sank down to the bed, filling my chest with power and pride as he drank in the sight of my near-bare chest.

"You're beautiful."

"You've barely seen me," I insisted, feeling a blush spread down my chest and to my thighs. He slid a hand over my leg and my stomach; I swallowed hard, trying to be patient but eager for the pressure of his hand between my legs.

"I've seen enough to know," he said.

"You've seen enough?"

He realized his mistake. "Uh… no. Definitely not."

I grinned, appreciating the way his brain seemed to stall. Was I really *that* attractive? I'd never felt particularly ugly, but right now I felt like a goddess. Like I somehow matched the way he made me feel.

But that couldn't possibly be true. Could it?

"Can I…?" His fingertips strayed to the front of my pants.

"Yes."

Every gesture was careful. When he leaned close to kiss me again, catching my lips like I'd starved him of my touch for hours, I knew exactly how he felt. My body was practi-cally aching with the desperation. Whether his hands were slow out of shyness or respect, I couldn't wait much longer.

"Preston, I… *please*."

He pulled back, eyes roving over me — catching on the strip of see-through lace at the waistband of my panties. It drove me wild to see him look at me like that. I teased my hand through the stripe of premature silver in his hair, and groaned as he leaned in to plant a soft kiss over the fabric between my legs.

"Preston," I begged.

"Sorry," he said, nuzzling his face into my thigh. "You're just... wow. You're a lot to look at." With an apologetic grin, he shuffled back up the bed to wrap his arm around me and kiss me again, letting me wrap one leg around him. I could feel his hard cock straining for me.

"This isn't too fast for you?"

"God, no," I said — and it was true. I'd never moved so quickly before in my life, but I'd also never been so sure. I didn't feel vulnerable in the arms of this strong soldier, even knowing how easily he could snap me in half. I didn't feel shy or degraded at the thought of his eyes on my naked body. Even as he unclasped my bra and swallowed as it fell away, entranced by the sight of me, I could only read desire in his eyes. There was nothing holding me back, and only snow-balling desire pushing me forward.

He gave me his hand first, his fingers arched and breath-takingly gentle as he lifted the fabric at my crotch aside. Every time his flickering touch increased, I thought I might lose myself then and there, before he even filled me — but then his touch would lighten again, and pull back, and lower me to a desperate, melting simmer. By the time he finally reached up to slip my panties down, lifting my leg up high on his hip, I was barely coherent.

"You tell me how you want it," he murmured, his forehead pressed to mine. "Don't let me hurt you."

I'd rather that than wait a second longer, I thought. Instead, I said, "Yes. Just... yes."

I'd never been so ready without lubricant. When he slipped inside me, hot and tight and willingly eager, I gasped and arched into him, feeling exactly how deep his cock curled inside me. He gave me a couple of slow, gentle moments to adjust, rolling his hips to let me feel the shape of him — then, careful and strong still, he shifted me onto my back and kissed the breathlessness out of me.

"You're beautiful," he said again. Then he thrust into me, still slow enough to feel every electric sensation. He slipped a hand between us to tease at my stomach, my nipple, my clit — I lost track of his fingertips in the shared body heat and the way his cock felt, driving all sensible thought out of my mind.

It was incredible to be had like this — gentle like a long-term lover, but with all the spontaneity and excitement of a first time. He had me shuddering to a prickly-hot climax within minutes. Then another — and once he finally came in me, deep and groaning and handsome as in old Hollywood despite the tattoos and the piercings, he didn't get up yet. He pulled out and lay close to me, sharing my breath as that slick, talented hand worked me to one last mounting, desperate orgasm, my hand gripping death-tight at his hard-working arm.

I felt his fond, soft kisses. I knew that I was curling up against him, dizzy with heat and exhaustion. Then I lost track and fell asleep in the comfort of his arms and the scent of his hair.

It wasn't just the way he loved me that felt familiar. Everything that filled my senses was like a husband I'd forgotten about — some lover from a parallel world that I'd never met before. I knew the feel of his skin on mine, and his heartbeat; the sound of his sighs, and the taste of his lips as he kissed me back awake.

"You okay?" he asked. "Seemed like I tired you out there."

"You did," I admitted, suddenly a little shy now that I was out of the eye of the storm. "That was… wow. *Wow*, Preston."

He smiled. I saw shyness in him too, and it steeled me. When he leaned to kiss me again, catching my lips in another sweet kiss, I felt a little more assured.

This was right. It just *was*, somehow.

We dressed slowly, showered separately, and somehow got back to our day. If he was a little more touchy with me, then that was only a pleasant thing — and I had to bat his hands away every time I started cleaning something away, as though he felt awkward about letting me do my job now that we were newly intimate. For as normal as it felt between us, though, we didn't have any discussions about it.

Were we *something* now? It felt like it, but we'd made no promises. He hadn't even mentioned the other guys, but the thought of them now made me guilty. That was foolish, wasn't it? As though any of them would want me anyway. The fact that Preston did was incredible enough. I couldn't cause any fights.

Still, it felt like a bad idea to tell them — even Stone, who I had been friendliest with. If Preston told them about it, then I wouldn't mind, but I already resolved to keep my part in this to myself.

Where it led from here, I couldn't possibly say. I just knew that the way he looked at me was exciting, and that my heart skipped a beat at the thought of finding another opportunity for him to touch me again.

see she's in your thoughts a lot.
Ah, shut up. Sir.

I tossed my head as we ran, letting out a growling ripple of laughter from my lion's throat. Stone only called me *Sir* on a couple of rare occasions — and embarrassment was one of them. Clearly, accidentally transmitting Jessica's face to me as we communicated had him feeling a little awkward, but he didn't have to.

Not least because if I didn't have good self-control, I'd be doing the exact same thing to him.

We might have to cut this short if we catch sight of anything, but... would it surprise you to hear that she's caught my eye too?

She has?

I heard the thunder of Stone's paws pick up behind me, and slowed so that he could pull alongside. I had never been good at reading people, either in this form or in our human ones, but Stone had a knack for it. Whatever he saw in my dark lion's eyes, it must have convinced him that I wasn't joking.

Ever since we'd come here with Jessica, I'd suspected that

something unusual was going on. I could feel my own pulse rising around her, and that hormonal shift. She was beautiful, of course, and the light behind her eyes gave her an air of easy confidence and happiness. When I looked at her, I saw a healthy, responsible and charming woman that spoke to every part of me — my lion included.

If the others were thinking the same thing… well. She might just be a myth come to life. Normally I'd dismiss the very idea of the one true mate, as I had done for years, but it wasn't so easy to do that with Jess. The very sight of her made me believe in the possibility. If anybody could be that special person — for anyone, but our pride in particular — it'd be her.

Really, though? Stone pressed again. *I don't want to cause a problem with us.*

It's not a problem, I said. I hadn't realized how true this was until this very moment. The weight of the fact came to rest on my back slowly, and I slowed to walk beside Stone, paws deliberate and heavy on the ground. This was a good thing, and the way I could feel my lion's heart throbbing in my chest only emphasized that — but it was pretty seismic.

Stone turned his head to face me, his dark eyes meeting mine. *Are you sure, Blake? You know I'd never—*

I think she may be our One Mate.

We both stopped. Stone's eyes rooted on mine, a flash of human depth in his expression. If he were with anybody else, he might have expected this to be a joke, but I wasn't really the joking kind. Not about things like this. I saw the realization wash over him, as it had just washed over me a couple of seconds ago.

He shifted, and I saw the same look of bemusement and confusion on his human form's face. I shifted to join him, sitting down on the warm dusty ground.

"If that's true, then…" Stone trailed off, shaking his head

down at the ground. "I can't believe it. I was never even convinced they existed. I'm not sure I'm convinced even now."

"I'm not jealous of your attraction to her," I reasoned. "Or the thought of her being attracted to you. Considering how long we've known her and how little time we've spent together, I'd say it's unusual to be so attracted to her."

"I guess so." Stone ruffled a hand through his hair, eyes unfocused. "Have you spoken to the others about it?"

"Not yet," I admitted. "It only crossed my mind in passing before, but I've seen them looking at her too and suspected it. Feeling her cross your mind so much with nothing else to distract me just… provided me with the evidence I needed."

"Wow."

We sat in silence for a few moments, feeling the wind lift around us. If our lion noses hadn't been clear of the scent of humans around us, then it probably wouldn't be safe to do this — but with the area around us so desolate and empty, and with shrubs and trees surrounding us for cover, it was a harmless spot to recover from this emotional earthquake.

"She's going to need to know," said Stone, after a few moments. "Everything."

I nodded, staring off into the distance. "We'll talk about it. All four of us."

"It's going to scare the shit out of her." His brow was furrowed with concern.

"No," I said, rolling my shoulders back and preparing to shift again. "No, it shouldn't. Not if she's the One."

STONE

It was hard work keeping my eyes off her. Now that I knew what Jess was to me, and to all of us, it was even harder than before to contain myself. Only a few feet from me she was humming away, absent-minded, and cleaning the kitchen counter tops. If I stood up and walked over to her and asked, she'd probably give me a hug; she was a tactile person, and I could already imagine pressing up against her, my nose filling with the scent of her berry-fresh shampoo and the smooth silk of her skin.

I swallowed, staring down at the table as she moved to another counter, afraid that she'd speak to me. Right now, I wasn't confident I could speak without making a damn fool out of myself. How could I, knowing that I was looking at the woman I was destined to be with? Knowing that one day she'd bear our children, and create the kind of family most lions could only picture in their dreams?

"I don't know how you all do it."

I looked up, attention snatched by the sound of her voice. As I tried to focus on not speaking to her, it was almost like I'd forgotten she could speak to *me*.

I blinked, a smile tugging onto my lips instinctively. She just had that effect on me.

"Do what?" I asked.

"All these shifts," she said, nodding towards the bedroom. "You seem to sleep and wake up at different times every day."

"It's either that or two of us don't see the sun for a couple of months," I pointed out. "And while I'm sure Preston would love that, I-"

A crash outside cut me off. Blake was already climbing to his feet and heading to the window, gesturing to me with one hand. He didn't need to ask me twice — and despite the vagueness of the gesture, I knew exactly what he meant.

"Jess, get down behind the counter."

"What…?"

I stepped to her side, looking over Blake's shoulder through the window. I couldn't see anything outside. Judging by the way Blake grimaced and moved to the door, neither could he. I touched Jess's shoulder gently, guiding her down. Any other time, this would have been contact I'd have fixated on, but right now we didn't have time.

"Keep down, okay? We don't know what that was."

I followed Blake outside, eyes narrowed as I stared out to the line of trees nearby. Blake had already shifted and seemed to have scented something. His eyes were trained directly ahead, and I could hear the beginnings of a growl rippling through his throat.

Get Jess below ground. Wake the others. We have some unfriendly visitors.

On it, I confirmed in my head. If there were enemies around, I didn't intend to give anything away out loud.

As soon as I was back inside, I closed the door behind me and waved Jess over. "Keep low," I said, lifting the rug to reveal the entrance to the basement below — our safe room. "I don't know who's out there, or how many. Grab my sweater from the couch; it'll be cold down there. I'm going to get the others."

Walking away from her was hard. I could see the tremors in her hands and the fear and uncertainty in her eyes — but I knew the best thing I could do to keep her safe was to follow Blake's instructions so we could neutralize the threat. Staying with her wouldn't do that.

Still, it didn't make it any easier to leave her behind. I gritted my teeth, and pushed into Hale and Preston's room.

"Hat up, guys. We've got company."

JESSICA

Of course, I knew the North boys were working on something dangerous, in a vague sense. I understood that it was risky — but to actually have the fight come to our little cabin like this was imminent and frightening. I could no longer kid myself that I was completely safe here, even if it was obvious that the boys had every intention of protecting me.

I didn't really like the idea of being protected, normally. I wasn't the type to wait for a knight in shining armor if I could take care of business myself. Woe betide the old-fashioned creep at the grocery store who assumed I couldn't carry my own bags out to the car — but this? This was way beyond my scope. It was beyond the scope of any civilian. Judging by the way the boys were reacting, they hadn't exactly been expecting it either.

Down in the basement by myself, I pulled Stone's sweater tighter around my shoulders. He was right. It was chilly down here, but I had a feeling that most of my shivering had to do with something else entirely. Were they safe out there?

Less pressing, was I safe down here?

Hearing nothing from the cabin above, I could do nothing but wait. My mind ran over with thoughts of the worst-case scenarios, imagining the smirking faces of the enemy peering down at me from above. Or maybe they wouldn't know I was here and would burn down the cabin around me — either consigning me to suffocation, or to dying of thirst in the wilderness as I tried to seek out help.

I couldn't guess how much time had passed when the hatch at the top of the basement steps finally opened. Knees tucked up to my chest, I craned my neck to look up, suddenly assaulted by the thought that the attackers had won.

Instead, Blake's handsome face looked down at me, somehow calm despite the sweat on his brow and the mud on his clothes.

"All safe," he said, barely out of breath. "You can come on up now."

"Are you all okay?" I asked as I climbed to my feet, my legs strangely unsteady as I made my way up. I felt so childish and weak. So delicate. "I couldn't hear anything down here."

"Everyone's fine," he promised. "I'm sorry we had to leave you by yourself down there. Just a precaution, you understand, but... we couldn't have risked you getting hurt up here."

"Did they reach the cabin?"

"No," he said, holding out a hand as I came within reach. "Not even close."

Still unsteady, I relented and took it. Even just the contact with his skin comforted me; I could feel his calming influence flowing through me like firelight warmth after walking in the snow. Now my heart was pounding for an entirely different reason than fear.

That said, fear still remained. "But they know where we are...?"

"Yes. But they won't come back. I don't want you going outside any time soon, but... they will not come back."

Instinctively, I wanted to ask how he knew that. They were the enemy, after all. Surely, they'd stop at nothing to wipe out the threat that the North boys posed — and me, by association, if they ever found out I existed? Maybe they'd been spying on us for a while, and already knew. Even as logic assailed me with all those worries, my mouth failed to follow suit. There was so much confidence and certainty in Blake's eyes that some deeper part of me just chose to believe him.

I realized that we were still holding hands, even as I stood at the top of the stairs. Around me, the others were coming down from the force of the attack. Stone was cleaning up a nasty-looking scrape on one of Hale's arms, not without their usual playful banter.

Blake squeezed my hand, drawing my eyes back to him. I felt my cheeks flush.

"It's okay, Jessica. I promise. If I believed it wasn't safe for you to be here, I'd take you straight home. Trust me."

"I do."

And though I'd only known him for a while, and though my instincts screamed that it was crazy to stay here, on a deeper level it was true. I *did* trust Blake. I trusted him enough that his hand in mine, solid and sensible and careful, was enough to soothe away the blindness and terror of that stretch of lonely time in the dark.

BLAKE

When I woke up in the middle of the night, it wasn't too unusual. There was a lot on my mind, and I didn't need much rest to get by. What *was* unusual was the sensation I had of discomfort. That there was something else I had to do before I went back to sleep.

I frowned and swung my feet out of bed. The air still carried a light scent of iron-rich blood. Ordinary human noses were not so sensitive, but it still felt wrong to keep Jessica in such a violent environment — safe though it was. I made my way out of the room, closing the door quietly behind me so as not to disturb Stone. I wasn't even sure what I was heading out to do before I caught sight of her.

Jessica was standing at the end of the corridor, leaning on the sill to look out of the window into the darkness. From the light glow of the candle beside her, I could make out the shape of the torn bodies of our attackers in the yard — left deliberately, to discourage any further attempts.

"Is that them, out there?" she asked, voice soft and quiet.

I was surprised that she'd noticed me. Even more so that

she didn't sound openly horrified at the thought of it. Instead, she sounded numb. Distant.

"It is," I confirmed. Only then did she look over her shoulder to take me in, the thin straps of her night dress not offering much protection against the nighttime cold. I could see the skin on the back of her neck raising and resisted the urge to touch her — to warm her up with my shifter's higher body temperature. Instead, I kept my distance. Let her keep her space as she turned back to face the dark.

"It looks like a bobcat got to them or something," she noted. "Maybe something even bigger. You sure it's okay to leave them out there?"

"There's nothing that can get inside," I assured her. She picked up the candle, lingering a few more seconds before she looked my way. "I promise. You're safe here."

"It's you boys I'm worried about," she said. "I didn't know there was such dangerous wildlife out here."

The knowledge that I'd have to tell her the truth about our nature swelled up in me, but this wasn't the time. Stone and I hadn't even had a chance to talk to Hale and Preston about it all yet.

"We'll be fine," I said. "What about you? You okay? Can't sleep?"

"That's a lot of questions."

She smiled at me, and I felt my built-in stiffness begin to ease away. I didn't spend much time with Jess alone, and doing so now only made me more certain that she was our one mate. I could practically feel my lion calling out to her from inside me, lifted up by the sight of her smile.

"I'm fine," she answered, after she saw me smile back. "I mean… I'm not. It was scary being down there. Imagining what might be happening to all of you. It shook me, but I'll be okay."

"Probably best not to look outside in the light," I suggested. "It's a mess out there."

"Think I'd have been standing at this window so long if I was squeamish?"

Jessica had a point, but it only raised another question. "How long *have* you been here?"

She sighed. "Too long. I meant to get a drink, but I just got… stuck, I guess."

I tipped my head towards the kitchen. "C'mon. Go have a seat in there. I'll make you something."

"I can get myself a glass of water," she insisted, bumping her elbow into mine as she passed me. Her eyes caught on my bare torso, her playful smile melting into something a little less guarded — a little less measured. Clearly, she liked what she saw; it encouraged me to meet her gaze, and skim my eyes over her body too.

"I'm sure you can," I said, delayed. "But let me do this for you. You just… rest."

Whether she was actually convinced or just knew I wouldn't give up the fight, Jessica relented and made her way to the couch, peering over the stiff back cushions to watch me fill the glass. Even in the low light, her blonde hair still shone, and there was an otherwordly glow to her skin.

No doubt about it. She was *my* mate. It didn't surprise me that the others felt this way too.

"Sorry," she said, sinking back behind the cushions a little as I caught her looking.

"What are you sorry for?"

I made my way over, and took the seat beside Jessica on the couch as I handed her the water. She seemed almost hesitant — not afraid of me, but not quite comfortable with me either. I shifted away, just a fraction, but she leaned right in to make up the gap.

"I don't know," she admitted. "You're just kind of intimidating, I guess."

She hadn't taken a drink yet. The condensation formed against the glass, and her eyes remained focused on mine. I tried to soften my smile, leaning back against the back of the couch.

"I don't try to be."

"I know," she said. "It's just a natural thing. Hale is the same way."

"Not the others?"

She gave me an awkward smile, hiding behind the glass. She must have been paying attention to all of us. That was a good sign. "Not in the same way, no. Stone feels like... I don't know. He's more approachable, somehow. And Preston is just... Preston."

"He's quiet, huh? Soft."

"To a point."

Jessica angled herself towards me a little more. Did she even know she was doing it? I turned too, elbow perched on the back of the couch to hold up my head. She was only a foot or two away from me.

"Well, I'm sorry for being unapproachable."

"It's not that," she insisted, cheeks blushing up. "You didn't do anything wrong."

I hummed, watching as she finally remembered the glass of water was for drinking instead of hiding behind, and the way her full lips pressed against the rim as she drank. "I guess I can be a little over-serious, though."

"You just have a lot of responsibility."

"We all do, really," I said, not wanting to take credit away from the rest of my pride. "But yeah, I do. I'm glad you understand. I don't want to be unfriendly to you."

"I certainly wouldn't say that."

My eyes drifted down to her upturned palm, sliding across the couch cushion towards me. Unthinking, I took it, and felt the warmth of her hand in mine — the spark of attraction that flew between us. I rested my thumb on her wrist, touch light enough to feel the rhythm of her pulse as it lifted and quickened.

"We're all so lucky to have you here," I told her. Even though I knew the others would never listen in I still kept my voice low, saving what I said just for her. "*I'm* lucky to have you here, even if I'm not too good at showing it."

Jess smiled. For a second, I thought I'd said too much too soon. She kept her silence, just holding my eye contact for a few beats. Then she gave my hand a gentle squeeze and shifted closer beside me, her side pressing into mine.

My arm shifted over her shoulder, natural and fond. The longer we spent curled up together, voices too quiet to disturb the night, the more that contact felt something more than fond. I could feel my whole body pulling towards her, both human and lion. I was a 30-year-old man, and this wasn't the first time I had been close to a woman like this. Far from it — but there was something different about her. Something in her scent that drew me to her. Something that promised there was more than a physical connection building between us, even in our comfortable silence.

"You've been so kind to me," she said, after a while. The empty glass lay forgotten on the table, light reflecting off the rim — and her eyes. It took me a beat to notice that I was staring, falling forward into the blue.

"You deserve a lot more than kindness."

It wasn't supposed to be a euphemism, but I saw her smile widen, slow with shy restraint, and matched it. If she wanted to take it that way, I wouldn't stop her.

"I'd like a lot more," she admitted.

I leaned back, feeling her follow me into the space. When she climbed across my lap, I felt the weight of her body press into my lap — felt my cock stir to attention underneath her, unrestrained in the loose fit of my sweatpants.

She gasped, rocking her hips against me. The strap of her night dress fell down over one shoulder, and I leaned to kiss the bare skin it left, tasting the night air on her body.

"Blake…"

"I don't want to rush you," I said, even as my heart pounded against hers. Even as I could feel my lion stirring. Eager. *Desperate.* "If you want to go slow. If this isn't what you want…"

"I want it. I do."

Without a second more to waste, I pressed our foreheads together, drinking in the moment. I wanted to savor the sensation of being close to her for the first time, but I couldn't wait for long before nudging her nose with mine, and meeting her lips for a deep, long kiss.

I could feel her melting against me — the light pressure of her chest against mine, her nipples forming soft peaks below the thin fabric of her night dress. I could feel her breath picking up as we kissed, and her hands raking through the short sides of my hair.

"God," she said, pulling back a little and cupping my face. "What are you doing to me?"

"I haven't even started," I said. I slid my hands up her thighs, fingertips creeping beneath the soft cotton of her night dress. Jessica shivered closer, knees tightening around me. My hands traveled further up, and I let her shuddering breath guide me to continue, feeling her lean closer and the hot air of her breath against my neck as my fingertips ghosted the front of her panties.

"*Blake…*"

I groaned, catching her lips again as I rode the sensation of her friction against my cock. She ground down into me, keening and moaning. When she let her dress fall away from her top half, pooling at her waist and exposing the soft, smooth mounds of her breasts, I leaned forward to kiss them. "You're beautiful."

Her hands trailed down, leaving a line of fire across the sharp-cut lines of my abs. I could tell what she wanted even before she began tugging at my waistband. Taking her weight, I lifted both her and my hips so that she could tug my sweatpants down, and relished in the eager gasp I heard as she found nothing but skin underneath.

"God! You're so big. I want you so bad."

Without my sweatpants between us, I could feel her panties damp against my cock. She was desperate now, arching her back and rocking down into me.

"Fuck, Jessica. You're so wet."

She moaned, lifting one of my hands down to guide it to the crotch of her panties. I rubbed a small circle over the front of her sex, enjoying the rippling sounds of her pleasure, and then pulled the fabric gently aside.

"Please, Blake. I can't wait any more."

I kissed her again, humming my agreement, and only broke away to guide my cock to her entrance. I lifted her slightly, ears tuned to the soft staccato of her enjoyment, and let her come down on me. Felt the sweet heat of her — the perfection of sliding together.

"Oh, *God*, Blake…"

She was already moving on me, rolling her hips forward to ride her pleasure out of me. I would have given her anything she wanted, and wouldn't stop her for the world — so I kept my hands on her hips, carefully guiding and lifting her as she loved herself on my cock.

Even now, it felt like more than sex. When I saw the

bounce of her breasts, or the red flush across her collarbones, or caught a glimpse of her beautiful sex, it took my breath away. It was so much more than the physical pleasure we felt — and it was *we*. I could feel her excitement magnifying mine. Knew that I couldn't feel good unless she did.

Her eyes fluttered shut, head tossed back as she rode herself closer to her peak.

"*Mmm.*"

"Yeah, Jessica," I said, massaging at her hips with tight hands. "God. Just like that. You're so fucking perfect."

I could have lost myself just watching her. I almost did, but only when she came did it finally push me over — only when her eyes screwed up tight, mouth falling open as her back arched hard, body clenching around me and shuddering with the intensity of her pleasure. I came too, thrusting up inside her with a quiet groan of pleasure, and holding her there close against me. We were close enough to kiss, but for a few long moments we just caught our breath, noses pressed together and with her arms wrapped tight around me.

"Oh my god," she said. The tension in her body loosened and she shifted forward against me, suddenly loose and soft against my bare chest. I wrapped my arms around her, holding her close as I felt her heartbeat finally begin to slow.

"Uh-huh," I agreed. After all these years of searching, I'd never felt such an intense connection before, not least the first time I'd been with a woman. I didn't want to let her go. Didn't feel like she wanted me to. I kissed the cool dampness of her forehead, and let my mind focus on the rise and fall of her chest — the squash of her breasts against me. "You are… absolutely perfect."

"No," she insisted, nuzzling into my shoulder — but I could feel her smiling, and I smoothed my hands over the small of her back.

"Yes," I insisted. "Perfect. Just… incredible."

Sometime in the night, I'd have to take her back to her room. We couldn't wake up in the morning, still surrounded by the scent of sex, as the other North men made their way through the room — but for now, at least, we could just stay like this, wrapped up in each other. Wrapped up in the moment. At peace.

HALE

The more time passed by, the more all of our lives began to revolve around Jess. Though we hadn't had time for the group meeting Blake wanted until today, it was growing increasingly obvious that we all felt the same way about her — and that none of us were jealous about that. When she smiled at Preston, or touched Stone's shoulder as she reached for something beside him, it felt just as natural as it did when she blushed at me.

It also felt particularly obvious that we were all beginning to worry about her. Those smiles and blushes didn't seem so frequent any more. It could still be the attack frightening her, I figured. It had been less than a week. Still, there was a palpable concern in the air.

I didn't know whether she could be our One Mate, or if this was just a wild coincidence. It wasn't my call to make. But judging by Blake's decision to have us meet outside today, where Jess couldn't hear us, I could begin to guess.

We stopped in the woods. At intervals of ten meters or so, there were scattered remains to remind our one-time attackers that they were not welcome here. It was unlikely

that they'd return, but we all had our guard up in any case —
noses filled with the rusted metal scent of old blood, and the
occasional cloying hint of decay.

Our eyes all fell on Blake, waiting for him to speak.
Normally I'd be making a joke, but now didn't seem like the
time to fool around.

"Alright," he said, looking between all of us. "We should
talk about Jessica."

"She seems… low," said Stone, not missing a beat. It didn't
surprise me that he was first to speak up. As much as we all
adored her, she and Stone had been totally comfortable
around each other right from the very beginning. "That's my
main concern."

"I agree," said Blake, holding up a hand. "But I also want
to make sure we're all on the same page here. We're all
feeling something for her."

Stone nodded, eyes focused and intense. Preston nodded
too — but slower, and more deliberate. He cleared his
throat.

"I want to be upfront," Preston said. "We slept together.
About a week ago, once I wasn't so sick. It just kind of…
happened. It felt right."

My heart flipped. I felt no jealousy whatsoever — just a
prickle of excitement that she felt comfortable enough to be
with Preston like that. To think that sometime soon, she
might want to be with me too.

Preston's eyes darted between all of us, checking for signs
of anger or displeasure. He didn't find any. Instead, Blake
nodded.

"Me too."

"You have?" Stone blinked. If I didn't know him so well, I
might think there was a little envy in his tone, but I heard
that uptick in his voice for what it was: surprise. "When?"

"The night of the attack," said Blake. "She was awake,

standing at the window. Of course, I had to make sure she was okay, and… one thing led to another."

"I think I understand, then," said Preston. "I assumed she was scared of another attack, but… maybe she just feels guilty. Hasn't really been looking at me so much recently."

"Of course," I piped up. "She wouldn't know what the hell a One Mate is even if she *did* know we were shifters. She'd just feel like she was… I don't know, going behind our backs. She probably has no idea what the hell's going on with her."

Stone's lips pressed into a firm line. "We've got to tell her."

"Right now?" I scrubbed at my jaw, unconvinced. "I don't know. If she's already down, what's a shock like that going to do to her? I think we should wait. Maybe she'll get an instinct for it. Not the shifter stuff, but… with the four of us, at least."

"Somehow," said Preston, "I don't think it's as easy as that. For all we know, she thinks that being with multiple guys is immoral whether it's with permission or not."

"Some humans do it," Stone pointed out.

"But not all of them." Blake folded his arms. His voice had that tell-tale firmness; he'd made his decision, and as pride alpha, we were instinctively ready to follow. "Preston is right. Monogamy is pretty much the default setting for humans. She may already feel like she's doing something wrong; I don't want to overwhelm her with expectations. Let's just take it easy and give her some time to come to terms with everything so far. Give her some space. Yes?"

Preston and I nodded. Stone did too, but his eyes were cast down at the ground, and his lips set in a worried line.

"Hey," said Blake, voice strong but kind. "She'll be okay. She's tough, and we're still going to be there for her. I just think it's too much to put it all on her in the first couple of weeks she's here. That's all."

"It's not that I'm impatient," Stone insisted. He opened his mouth to continue, but closed it again as Blake held up a hand.

"I understand," said Blake. "I know you. I know you're looking out for her. I just think this is best for now. We'll see how things develop from here. We're not going to leave her to wallow in guilt. Okay?"

Stone nodded again, a little firmer this time. "Okay." But as we headed back to the cabin, he evidently wasn't thrilled — and honestly, I wasn't either. Blake's decision was probably best. I could see the logic of it, and I knew he was right not to overwhelm her. Still, the image of Jess chewing on her lip and staring off into space, consumed with confusion and guilt, didn't rest easy on any of our shoulders — human or lion.

JESSICA

The North boys seemed to have noticed that something was wrong with me, and they were all being characteristically kind — but frankly, their sweetness only made me feel worse. Not only had I slept with Preston while harboring a crush on all four of them, but now I had also slept with Blake. It was probably only a matter of time before they found out, and it would hurt them.

And it would all be my fault.

This wasn't something I had ever done before. Ordinarily I felt bad about dating several guys at once; I had certainly never slept with two close best friends like this. The fact that it was only a matter of days apart didn't make me feel any better. Even at the time, however, I felt I couldn't control myself. In the moment, it felt like the most right and natural thing in the world to fall into Blake — just like it had been with Preston. Now that I was in my own mind and away from the heat of the moment, it seemed insane, but at the time I recalled a feeling of purpose. A depth of emotion that I shouldn't be experiencing so soon after I had met these men.

Physically, I could have pulled myself away, but I didn't wanted to. Not in the least. Not in either case.

Even now, looking back as I finished up with my skincare routine, I couldn't look my reflection in the eyes and honestly say I regretted it. It was bizarre, and I hated myself for it. I had always believed I was a better person than this, and now here I was risking pain for these guys that I adored so much. Now here I was, melting at the seams the second their handsome smiles landed on me.

Speaking of the devil — in the mirror reflection, I caught sight of Stone hovering at my open door. I met his eyes and smiled as he knocked on the frame.

"Hey," I said, trying to iron out any sadness or frustration in my voice. Sure, they had already worked out that something was wrong with me, but I had no intention of making it any more obvious. "You're lucky. You just missed seeing the green face mask."

"Sounds pretty unlucky to me," he reasoned, stepping in. "You got a couple of minutes?"

"For you?" I said. "Sure. You can have exactly 120 seconds."

His grin twitched at the corner, lopsided, and he took a seat on the edge of the bathtub. "I guess that'll be enough. I just... kind of wanted to check in on you. Make sure you were doing okay."

Subtle, I thought. Still, it was a kind gesture. I wasn't about to scare him off for daring to care about me. "I'm fine," I said. "Just doing my skincare."

"Yeah, I meant in a more general sense than... the present thirty seconds."

I looked over my shoulder to meet him in the eyes head on, not just in the reflection. Those brown eyes were so warm and sincere that it was difficult not to spill out every welled-up feeling I had, but I knew that was a recipe for disaster. I forced myself to turn back to my own reflection, and hoped that my smile wasn't as obviously fake to Stone as it was to me. "Well. I have a good relationship with my family. I have plenty of friends. I *did* just quit my job to come and work with you guys on a whim, so that *might* be a sign of some kind of mental break…"

"You seem like you're having a hard time with something," said Stone, tone blunt but fond. "I can see you're dodging me, so I won't push. But if you *do* want to talk about whatever it is, I hope you know I'm here."

"You're very sweet," I said, and meant it. The next part, not so much. "If I seemed off today, it's probably that I've had a headache."

"You have?" he said. I hadn't known Stone very long, but I already recognized the playful sarcasm. Clearly, he didn't believe me in the slightest. "Well, that's no good. Let me get you a Tylenol."

"No, I-"

"You can't just struggle through with a headache," he said, standing up from the bath. He held up his hands. "You leave me with no choice but to get off my ass and walk all the way to my medicine cabinet, and then to the kitchen to get you something to wash it down with."

"Stone."

"Look at all this effort I'm going to do on your behalf."

"Oh, stop." I couldn't fight the smile off my face any longer, and swatted at his arm with my hand. "Alright, alright. But you're right. I am dodging you, and I don't want to talk about it."

His triumphant smile softened, and he nodded. "Not the kind of thing I like being right about. Look, whatever it is. If there's anything I can do to help you, will you just promise to tell me? Doesn't matter what it is."

I don't know, Stone. Can you reach into the past and slap my hands away from your teammates?

"If you've got a magic pill to wash away stress," I said instead, "that would be nice."

He held up a finger. There was something light in his eyes, and right away I wondered what I'd triggered. "Hold on," he said. "Wait here."

"Stone, I was joking."

"Wait here!" he called back, already half-jogging out of the room. It dragged another weary smile back onto my face, and I turned back to the mirror to check that all my face cream was absorbed. Finding no issues, I headed back to my bedroom, and saw Stone returning with a small bottle in his hand.

"I really don't need-"

"Doctor's orders," said Stone, voice cheery, and tossed the little glass bottle to me. "This is lavender oil. Two drops on your pillow. Perfect for some restful sleep."

My heart swelled. I felt, instinctively, that Stone meant what he said. He'd do anything for me, just to make me feel even a single bit better. It made me want to tear up, but instead I felt a now-familiar tug in my stomach.

Oh. Not you, again.

"That's kind, Stone. Thank you."

"Now, doctor's *recommendation*," he said. "You can refuse this one, but... I give a mean back massage. Totally guaranteed to work out stress just as well as it works out knots."

I hoped I wasn't blushing too badly, but I could feel the heat gathering in my cheeks and on the back of my neck. "I mean. That's..."

"Up to you," Stone insisted. "I figure if I can't talk about whatever-it-is with you, I can at least get you comfortable enough to deal with it yourself."

I should decline. I knew that. I was already feeling guilty enough about having had both Preston and Blake's hands on me, and the prickling feeling of attraction I felt for them was here for Stone too. If he touched me, especially in such a kind and intimate way, I didn't know how it would escalate. Didn't know if I could stop myself.

What I *did* know was that I wanted it anyway, more than I could bear.

"I mean. Are you sure...?"

"Are you kidding?" he said. His face lit up. "Of course. I want to help, and I'm good at it. Look, I'll get some of this lavender oil on a pillow for you. You just... lie down and get comfortable."

If my blush wasn't fire-red before, it certainly was now. The backs of my ears were burning, but I tried to ignore that too-human mix of excitement and nerves as I laid down on the bed.

"Prop up on your arms," Stone suggested, his voice soft and easy. "That's it."

As I got settled, he slipped a pillow underneath my head. Sure enough, the soothing scent of lavender filled me — strong, but not overwhelming. I sighed, sinking back down into the pillow, and closed my eyes. "You're right. It is nice."

"See," said Stone. "I know some things."

"A couple, I guess."

I felt the weight of the bed shift as he climbed on. For a brief moment I felt my whole body flush with heat as I imagined him straddling my waist. It thrilled me so much that I was almost disappointed when he did the gentlemanly thing and sat on one side of me instead.

"Let me know if I go too hard," he said, voice soft.

"Psh," I said, muffled into the pillow. "You couldn't go hard enough if you tried."

I smiled at his laughter. As intensely attractive as Blake and Hale were, it was also nice to spend time in Stone's friendly, unassuming company. He was just as handsome, but his appeal was markedly different to theirs. It felt less like the exciting mystery of being with a handsome stranger, and more like the firelight familiarity of an old childhood friend who had grown up *very* right.

When he actually laid his hands on me, though, there was no 'too hard' or 'too soft'. Even over my pajama cami, every trail of contact felt perfect. Whether it felt wonderful because it was Stone or whether he really was as expert as he claimed, I wasn't sure. Either way, I never wanted it to stop — not even when I heard myself make a quiet moan I hadn't intended, feeling a knot of tension dissipate under the warm arch of his palm.

"You're welcome," Stone teased.

"You *are* good at this."

"Uh-huh. I'm good at a lot of things."

"I believe it," I assured him, eyes squeezing tighter shut as he worked another knot out of me. I never wanted him to pull his hands away. In fact, I wanted them to explore further — wanted them smoothing just as firm and eagerly over every private plane of my body. It was only as I heard him chuckle quietly that I realized my back was arching under his hands.

"Sorry," I mumbled, shuffling on the bed. If I could have made myself smaller, I would have, but Stone didn't seem to mind the blatant body language.

"I'll take it as a compliment," he said. I could still hear the laughter coloring his tone, but not in an unpleasant way. I could imagine the smile playing across his handsome face and spent every inch of energy I had on continuing to lie face-down. On *not* springing up to touch him back. Unfortunately, it seemed my body told the story anyway;

he spoke up again. "You okay? You seem tense all of a sudden."

"I'm fine. I swear."

Stone hummed, fingertips kneading the small of my back. It was heaven through the fabric. I could only imagine what it would feel like skin-to-skin.

"Well, I don't want to make you uncomfortable," he said. "So if you want me to stop…"

"You better not."

He laughed again, soft and sweet. I couldn't help but smile into my folded arms, as enchanted by his warm company as I was by his magic hands. As his thumbs worked a particularly potent bit of pressure into the small of my back, I couldn't wait any longer. In fact, I was barely conscious of making a choice as I rolled onto my back and sat up, fixing his eyes with mine.

Stone didn't speak. I could feel the rise and fall of my chest, and saw his rising and falling in unison. He seemed to be leaning closer, and I felt my shoulders moving towards him too — closing the gap between us in inching movements until my jaw was cradled in his hand, and his nose pressed up against mine.

"You sure about this?" he murmured. "I care about you, Jess. I don't want to rush you. Don't want to mess with your head."

I closed my eyes, tipping my chin towards his for a soft, deliberate kiss. "I'm sure."

He exhaled, lips hovering close to mine. His thumb brushed over the line of my jaw, careful and eager. "Because I want to, but if you don't-"

I reached into his lap, smoothing my hand over the front of his sweatpants. Beneath the fabric, I felt the hardening swell of his cock — and moments later, the forceful rush of his kisses. Apparently, there was no more uncertainty left.

He wrapped his arms around my waist as I climbed into the exquisite heat of his lap, rolling my body down against his cock. Here it was happening all over again — this powerful, cosmic force that made me forget any complaints I might have had, and made me desperate for his embrace. As he peppered kisses over my collarbone, fingertips dipping under the thin strap of my cami, I only had the capacity to breathe.

"I wanted you all this time," he admitted, lips close enough to tickle the skin of my neck as he spread his affection across my body. "Always hoped you'd want me too." His thumb flicked over the sensitive peak of my nipple, and he kissed up the gasp it drew from my lips. Heat pooled there beneath his touch, and further down between my legs.

"I did want you," I told him, albeit delayed; I felt the shape of his smile form against my skin, and soon his mouth lifted to mine again for another full, fond kiss. "I *do* want you."

"Lucky us."

He wrapped his arms around my waist, holding me close as I absorbed the flush and fire of his kisses. With Stone, this sexual magnetism didn't feel quite so wild or frantic; it was a different kind of passion, slower but just as white-hot. Though I wanted every inch of him, and couldn't help but ride the shape of him in his lap, I didn't mind that he held me up with kisses for such a long stretch of time. Didn't mind that it took him what felt like hours to tip me back against the pillows of my bed, and begin to crawl down my body.

He helped me shift off my pants, and took my white cotton panties down with them. When he leaned back down, eyes fixed on my sex like I was some kind of extraordinary work of art, I realized I was holding my breath.

"Thought about this a lot," he admitted, voice low and husky enough that I believed him. This was the realization of weeks of frustrated dreams for both of us — and now, writhing as I parted my legs a little wider, I gave a shuddering gasp as I felt him press those first few gentle kisses to my stomach — then lower, and less gentle.

He hummed his appreciation, his lips and tongue too occupied with the divine pressure and play on my body. Only after warming me up like this for a long time did he introduce his fingers to my slick entrance, teasing a series of escalating groans from me.

I took tight hold of his spare hand, enjoying the gentle tangle of our fingers as much as the much more intimate strokes of his tongue. "God, Stone…"

"It's good?" he said, the closeness of his breath had its own incredible sensation — just not quite intense enough. My toes curled, desperate for more.

"It's incredible. *You're* incredible. But aren't you…?"

"I want to let you come like this first," he said as though it were a confession, looking up at me under an almost bashful wave of blond hair. My heart skipped a beat. "Then I'll fill you up. If… that's what you want."

He had the luxury of sweet language; I did not. "God, yes. Fuck me."

Stone grinned, and I felt the spine-melting trace of his tongue over those sensitive nerve endings once again. His movements were quicker now, and more insistent; I felt the regularity of his rhythm begin to lift me up, heart pounding like an animal on the hunt and somehow more and more desperate the more imminent my orgasm seemed. I needed it now, and now, and *now* — impatient right up until the moment my toes tensed and my legs tangled around him, crying out and arching up in bliss into the sweet pleasure of his mouth.

"Mmm," he hummed, slowing his licks and kisses and diverting to less sensitive areas as I slid down from the precipice. "Exactly. Just like that."

"Stone, *fuck.*"

"Wow. Impatient," he teased, deliberately misinterpreting.

I grinned, tugging his hand to summon him closer, and grateful when he understood. I didn't want to have to expend any more breath on telling him where I wanted him — not when I could be kissing him instead, falling deep into the texture of his affection.

"That was good, huh?"

"Amazing," I mumbled, winding my hands into his hair. My grip felt weak, and I realized I'd been crumpling the sheets beneath us into balls of fabric in my hands. It was enough just to wrap my arms around his shoulders, feeling a new wonderful pressure as he lay on top of me. "God, god. Yes."

"Already?"

"*Please.*"

If he had been expecting me to recover before I had him, then he didn't know how good he was — hadn't even guessed it from the way my leg hooked around his, and how I tried to press my hips up into him. He was so hard now that there was no mistaking the shape of him in his sweatpants. When he sat up, I could see the full and clear outline of him straining through the fabric, even before he tugged them down and treated me to the sight of his thick, perfect cock.

"Mmm," I hummed, words failing me in the moment. He gave himself a few strokes, maybe showing off a little — but with a flushed grin on his face that only made me want him more. "God, please. I want you so bad."

Stone didn't make me wait much longer. After a few eager kisses on my neck, he leaned back to guide himself inside me, so thick and tight and *good* that my toes curled around his heel, heat flickering and spreading up through me from the base of my spine.

I melted into the pleasure, moaning into his shoulder.

His skin was already damp with heat, and I buried myself in him just for the scent. I wasn't really sure how pheromones worked, or hormones, or whatever the hell they were — but whatever hold his biology had over me, it was a potent force.

"God, you're beautiful," he murmured, turning his head to press a long, lingering kiss on my temple. "I can't believe how lucky I am."

"How lucky *you* are? *Ahh*, Stone—"

I arched hard as his cock moved deep inside me, shuddering around the spark of the sensation, and muffled my cries against his shoulder. All this waiting and dreaming and desperation, and it had finally come to this moment, more blissful than I'd hoped. I felt his heart beating in time with mine, hard and rapid inside his chest.

Before long, I felt his thrusts get a little more frantic — felt the desperation as he tipped his head back to find my lips and kiss me again through his shuddering, heavy orgasm. Soft and sweet no longer. Hand slipping down between us to rub at my clitoris with careful consistency, he made sure I followed not long after, kissing my sharp-edged cries of pleasure into muffled ones.

He couldn't stay all night. In fact, he didn't dare to stay for more than an hour; he didn't want to alarm Blake in case the alpha awoke to find Stone missing from his bed.

"He's pretty serious about stuff," he said, flashing me a lopsided grin of apology. "I'm sure you've noticed."

There was a flirtatious flicker in his eyes that pulled a tight knot in my stomach, making me wonder whether he already knew about my similarly wonderful trysts with Preston and Blake. If it was, he didn't say so, and kissed me a moment longer before crawling off the bed.

My heart was still pounding minutes after he'd left, long after it had slowed from the flurry of my orgasm. Living here felt like losing my mind one man at a time — and now that I'd slept with Stone too, that only left Hale lagging behind.

As I closed my eyes, feeling a wave of inexhaustible lust wash through me, I had already made up my mind.

I'd come this far. I wanted all four of them. If he'd have me, I needed to be with Hale too.

Having sensed Stone's animal glow as he came back from duty, I figured it must have happened for him. He finally had his moment with Jess. Wanting her like I did, I couldn't even bring myself to tease him about it. Instead, I just shot him a grin and patted his shoulder as I passed by. Saying something wasn't in my best interest, anyway. I knew I'd have the same light in my eyes the second I was lucky enough to take my turn, and then he'd be firing the same barbs right back at me.

If she really was the One Mate, of course.

It wasn't that I doubted it, per se. I knew how I felt when she blushed and looked away, too shy to hold my gaze; I knew the feeling of deep satisfaction that settled all over me whenever I helped her out in some small way. All the signs were strong — and maybe that was why I didn't dare to be sure. The idea that we'd found a One Mate at all was dizzying. For it to be Jess, and for it to feel like this?

Shit. I'd be crazy to let myself hope for it. If it didn't pan out, the disappointment would crush me.

Of course, I could try and think logically about all I wanted. Actually, resisting those feelings would be a different battle entirely. The second I stepped into the kitchen, hearing the door close on Blake and Stone behind me, I was caught up in the hourglass shape of her as she watched them walk away, and the unsteady rhythm her fingers drummed out on the counter-top.

I tapped her shoulder, stepping quickly to the other side before she could catch me there. Her smile was flustered, but sincere. She blushed right across the bridge of her nose, and tucked imaginary out-of-place hairs behind her ears.

"You're a born nuisance," she said, without any force or irritation whatsoever. Far from it. The quirk in the corner of her lips was full of warmth and light — despite the shyness. "Good morning, Hale."

"Morning, Jess. You sleep well?"

She turned her body away from the window now, leaning back against the kitchen counter. I was well-practiced at ignoring the swells of lust I felt around her now but seeing her hips arch forward a little against the surface drove me wild. I forced myself not to look directly, instead focusing on setting the coffee brewing.

"I did," she said. "For some reason I was extra-comfy last night. Like I was exactly where the universe wanted me to be right then. Is that weird?"

I swallowed. Lucky I was good at holding my composure. "Maybe?" I said, trying to sound casual. "But if it is, it's a good weird."

"I guess so."

Even now, she struggled to meet my eyes. I could see the blush had spread all the way down to her collarbone, and couldn't help but grin at her. "Aw, man. I still scare you after all this time?"

Jess tutted. "You don't scare me. I'm just... distracted, I guess. I have a lot to do today."

"Oh, right. Yeah." I smirked. As the coffee started brewing, I stepped back from the counter to give her a full look. No matter what she said, I could see that pretty glow of embarrassment on her. I figured I ought to take pity. "Well, don't let me keep you. I'm gonna head into the shower."

"Oh. Okay." I didn't know why this should be a surprise to her in the morning, but it sounded that way. Jess gave me a faint smile, shrugging her shoulders and turning back to the sink. "Well, you enjoy. I'll be right here."

I bit back a flirtatious invitation. She'd come to me on her own time, or not at all. Being playful and a little intimidating was one thing, but I absolutely did not want to risk making her feel pressured or uncomfortable. Whether she was our One Mate or not, I'd never treat her that way.

In my bathroom, I set the shower running. Preston was already awake and out training in the fresh air, so I didn't have to worry about being too loud; I could turn my speaker on and play the kind of high-energy music I needed to wake up properly. As the mirror began to steam up, I dropped my clothes in an unceremonious pile and stepped with an audible sigh into the water. With the combination of the intense pressure and heat of the shower and the background buzz of my music, I felt like I was coming back to life — and I hadn't even been too worn out to begin with.

For a military man, I had always been a little too prone to losing myself in showers. In ordinary service, I'd never get away with it. Here, in our little special ops cabin with our two shifts, it didn't matter so much that I closed my eyes and forgot how long I'd been under the spray. It didn't matter that I forgot about almost everything except Jess' warm smile and the curve of her ass until I heard a knock at the bathroom door.

"Yeah, come in," I called. I assumed it was Preston, needing something from the bathroom — but when the door opened it was Jess that appeared there, forcing herself to hold my gaze with a shy, brave smile.

"Hey."

"Well, hi." I couldn't contain my surprise, but I certainly wasn't embarrassed. She couldn't see anything immediately private thanks to the frosted glass at waist-height, and I sure didn't have a figure to be ashamed of. She seemed to like what she saw — but that didn't answer any of my questions. "You okay? You need something?"

"I, uh."

She cleared her throat. Only when she caught her bottom lip between her teeth did I realize that this wasn't a practical visit, and in a heartbeat our roles reversed. My jaw dropped a little, staring with unabashed intensity at the grin on her face.

"So, um. You want company?"

"You fucking bet I do."

I stepped closer to the glass, one hand up against the pane to get a better look at her. That blush was still present across the bridge of her nose, but she was working through the shyness. She even seemed to be enjoying it as she pulled her t-shirt up from the hem, revealing the smooth plane of her stomach inch by agonizing inch — then, as she lifted it high enough to reveal her soft, round breasts, I pressed closer to the glass with a quiet groan, feeling its pressure against the already-hard length of my cock.

Her eyes darted down, and her smile widened. "Oh. *Hi.*"

I grinned. "Yeah. Hi."

Maybe such an obvious sign of attraction helped her uncertainty to melt away. Maybe it was the confirmation she needed. Either way, when Jess' eyes met mine again, I saw only excitement in her face — not nerves.

"I should hurry up and get in there, huh?"

"Uh-huh. Water's real nice."

Her fingers dipped below the waistband of her yoga pants, peeling them slowly down until she could step neatly out. Now only the thin black cotton of her panties remained, but she didn't move to take them off just yet. Instead, she sank down into the bathroom chair, legs parted, and traced her fingertips over her stomach.

"Or maybe I'll make you wait a little longer."

I groaned, slipping a hand around the base of my cock for a few slow strokes, eyes rooted on her fingertips as they trailed an indeterminate path over her skin. Finally, *finally*, they made their way down inside her panties, and I swallowed hard as I heard her gasp.

"Fuck, Jess."

"Still think I scare you?" Her voice was already pitched up at the sharpness of her pleasure, and her laugh sounded breathy as I shook my head in silence. "You *are* intimidating. But it kind of makes me want to rise to the challenge."

"You're incredible," I told her, lifting a hand to wipe away the steam on the inside of the shower. I wanted a better look. *Needed* a better look. "So fucking beautiful."

Jess flicked a thumb over her nipple, and I watched as it peaked to a nub within a matter of seconds. That hand in her panties sped up a little; beneath the thin fabric, I could see her fingers teasing away in a circling motion.

"You've got to get in here," I pleaded. "You're driving me crazy."

"In a minute," she teased. "I want to be so ready for you."

I groaned, giving my cock a few more desperate strokes. "Yeah? You want me that bad?"

"Oh, yeah."

Her head tipped back as her breath shuddered, and I mapped out the spread of that beautiful blush of hers all the way down her chest — watched her toes curling, and the dampness of her skin in the humid heat.

When she stood up, I was so enraptured in watching her that it jolted me back into my senses. The water pounded down on my back as I kept my eyes rooted on her, drinking in the sight of her sex as she finally dropped her panties.

I opened the door, and watched her eyes fall straight to the unhindered sight of my cock. I groaned, pulling her close to me under the water for a deep, rough kiss.

"I can't wait," she said, fastening her arms around my neck. "God, please-"

"Fuck. C'mere."

I lifted her with the ease my military training gave me, and pressed her carefully up against the smooth tiles of the shower wall. The sensation of her nipples against my chest drove me wild, but she told me what she needed. I wasn't about to draw this out.

I reached down to my cock, aligned myself carefully with the joy-slick wetness of her sex, and pushed carefully inside.

Her shuddering groan spurred me on, her fingernails digging into the base of my neck and feet locked around me. Here in the shower, we didn't have much room, but neither did we need it. As I fucked her up against the wall, intimate and close, I kept a tight and steady rhythm that worked for both of us — me, deep inside her and surrounded by her heat, and she arched with pleasure at the feeling of fullness, and the careful pressure of my thumb on her clit.

"Oh, Hale. *God.*"

I buried my face in her neck, kissing and nipping wildly at the smooth, clean skin I found there. She smelled so good, with layers of hormones and personal scent, that I thought I'd lose my mind. Every cell in my body was celebrating this moment that I found her, and that I first had her.

I felt her toes curling and uncurling behind me, and the way she clenched around my cock in time with my thrusts. Her nails clawed down my back, stopping only when she spared a hand to cup my face and kiss me, deep and long. I could feel her moans vibrating against my lips as we kissed, and reveled in the thought of giving her all that pleasure. It wasn't long before those quiet moans turned into much sharper and more desperate cries.

"Hale, don't stop. Don't – *ahh...*"

The intensity of her orgasm gripped me, tugging me down over the edge with her. I came hard inside her, my thumb still circling a much gentler rhythm around her clit as she came down, breathing heavy and her forehead flopped against my shoulder.

"Wow."

"That good, huh?" I grinned, lifting a hand to smooth her bangs out of her eyes. The bun she'd tied it up in had gotten loose in the wetness, and it was good to see her face unobscured again — the deep, satisfied blue of her eyes.

"Mm." As I set her carefully down, keeping one arm loosely around her waist to hold her upright, I watched her place a hand carefully over my heart. Could she feel it racing still? I leaned down to kiss the top of her head, as happy to be close and soft with her in the shower as I had to see her naked body for the first time.

Oh, yeah. No doubt about it. This was the One Mate, alright.

We relaxed in comfortable silence, occasionally turning to help one another wash a different part of our bodies. It felt like we'd been together forever — not that we'd only just shared our first time in this tight-pressing space. Even me, notorious for never taking things seriously, couldn't ignore the welling happiness inside me.

This was our future now. Forever.

As we shut the water off and stepped out, sharing the comforting warmth of my hot, fluffy towel, it felt so natural to know that she'd be a part of whatever lay ahead of me.

I could hardly wait.

Time usually dragged out like crazy on these long-term missions — but this time, with Jess' glow to anchor and encourage us, it felt like the days had never passed more quickly. Before long, a whole month had flown by, and we had enough of the area scouted out that Blake predicted we'd find and contain our men within one more month.

This was good news, of course. We were doing important work that would keep our country safe — but despite this miniature victory in our mission, none of us felt all that triumphant. Although we were absolutely sure now that Jess was our One Mate, we still hadn't found adequate time to sit down all together and have a discussion about it. On top of that, Jess hadn't been quite herself for the past week or so, to the degree that Stone had insisted on calling in a doctor.

As she conducted the examination in Jess' private room, Hale and I sat in concerned stiffness at the dining room table.

"I don't know what to think," I admitted. "Obviously Stone didn't find anything, and I don't *want* there to be anything physically wrong with her — but what's the alternative?"

Hale shook his head, uncharacteristically serious. "Not good. The only other thing I can think of is that she found out we all know… you know. About all of us." He folded his hands together. "Maybe it upset her. Maybe she figured it was some kind of set-up. That it's the only reason we brought her here."

My chest ached at the mere thought of it, and I could see Hale struggling with it too.

"Nobody would've told her," I reasoned. "We agreed on that much. How else would she have found out?"

The question went unanswered. We fell back into silence until we heard the sound of Jess' bedroom door clicking open, and both her and the doctor's footsteps down the hallway.

"…Vitamin D, which will be sent along with the next supply shipment. Okay?"

"Sure. Thank you."

Hale and I stood from the table as they entered the room. I could feel his nervous energy echoing mine, and maybe Jess could too; she gave us both a weak smile as she caught our eye, and stood aside to let Doctor Gray pass.

"I'll let Jessica discuss it all with you," she said. "But there's nothing to be immediately concerned about."

"Thank you, Doc," said Hale. "We appreciate you coming down here."

"Hell of a drive," she admitted, adjusting her uniform collar. Even military doctors were used to being perfectly turned-out. "But you're doing good work here. I don't have details, but I've been told to inform you that your progress is better than anticipated. Least we can do is give you the support you need." She turned to Jess, giving her a soft smile. "Even if we don't have all the answers."

Ever the gentleman, Hale swept out an arm to lead her to the door. I stayed behind with Jess, fighting a growing feeling of unease. She looked so uncomfortable right now. The smile on her face was so forced and unhappy, and she wasn't looking up to meet my eyes.

"You okay?" I asked, voice low.

"Sure," she said. "I'm fine. Just... under the weather, I guess."

If anybody deserved not to be under the weather, it was Jess. Most of the time, she shined out like our own private sun; she lifted each of us up just by looking at us. It hurt to see her like this, even more so because I couldn't reach out and comfort the woman I knew was our One Mate. After all, *she* didn't know it yet.

"You'd tell us, right? If there was anything we could do for you?"

She nodded. "Of course. It's okay, Preston, honestly. I'm sure I'll be fine once these supplements arrive, like Dr. Gray said."

I wish I could believe it. Maybe the concern read too obviously on my face; her eyes dipped again as soon as she saw me, and she motioned towards the doorway with a weak smile. "Actually, if you don't mind, I think I'm gonna go lay down for a while. Laundry is already running and I don't need to start preparing dinner yet, so..."

"Hey, you don't need to justify yourself to me," I promised. "Please. Go lay down. Feel better."

I watched her go, taking a piece of my happiness with her. It seemed like nothing much was cheering her up right now. When Hale returned, I nodded in the direction of the bedroom.

"She okay?" he said, forming the words with unusual quietness and restraint.

"I don't know," I admitted. "She says so, but she seems real worn out."

"I doubt both Stone and Dr. Gray are missing something big," Hale reasoned. "They're both very competent." He paused. "Don't tell him I said that, obviously."

I gave him a weak smile. Usually Stone and Hale's banter was pretty entertaining to watch from the sidelines, but little could distract me from focusing on Jess right now. If Hale was being light-hearted as an attempt to take his own mind off of it, it clearly wasn't working. When he sank down into a dining chair again, his sigh was so heavy and world-weary that I barely recognized the sound of it.

"We're gonna have to schedule this meeting."

"With her?"

"Uh-huh."

I nodded slowly, considering. "Blake's call, of course."

"Sure," he agreed, as respectful of his alpha as any pride member could be. He always was when it really came down to it and mattered, however hard they played during the good times. That was one of the things I admired most about Hale. He always knew when to draw the line; he was just really good at pretending he didn't. "I'll talk to him when he gets back. Don't worry."

It was reassuring to have a plan — but having seen the downtrodden look on Jess' face just now, telling me not to worry was like telling a fire not to burn.

JESSICA

Is there any chance you could be pregnant?

An hour after Doctor Gray left the cabin, her question was still ringing in my ears. I wasn't some naive kid. Of course, I knew that unprotected sex could lead to pregnancy — and, with a flush of guilt, I knew it had been unprotected with all four North men. In the spur of the moment, that had felt like the right and natural thing to do. Now, if this was true?

The thought had me freefalling.

For one thing, I wouldn't know who the father was. For another, there'd be no chance of keeping my intimate moments with all four men a secret any longer. If they didn't already think I was cheap and easy, they probably would now. Even worse was the thought of sowing discord amongst this tight group of men I'd come to love so much. They worked so well together as a unit. Was I about to screw it up because I couldn't keep it in my pants?

I had made my excuses with Preston and Hale as soon as Doctor Gray left, heading back to my room for 'rest'. The pregnancy test she'd left behind for me sat on the countertop in the bathroom, intimidating in its sleek and clinical packaging. I'd never even taken one before. It scared me to think that this tiny cardboard box contained a stick that could change the rest of my life.

Well — no. That wasn't true. The test would just tell me the consequences of my own actions. Everything I had done was on me.

If any of my friends had come to me with this problem, I'd have fiercely insisted that they were only halfway to blame — if that. It took two to tango, after all.

Well, in this case, it had taken five, and I had no sympathy to spare for myself.

The longer I left it, the worse I was going to feel. Already I could practically feel the box's presence behind me when I turned my back; if I actually tried to sleep as I'd told Preston, I'd only end up lying there with my eyes closed imagining all the horrible possibilities. The anger and the hurt. What a horrible beginning for a new life.

Swallowing hard, I headed into the bathroom and closed the door behind me.

I knew you weren't supposed to stare at the thing while it developed. I knew it took a couple of minutes; I knew that watching it would only make the time pass more slowly. Still, I couldn't bring myself to look away, as though I'd blink and miss it. As though the result would disappear before I could see it.

Since it was impossible to distract myself with completely unrelated thoughts, instead I tried to soothe myself. For one thing, I loved babies. I had always imagined myself as a mom one day — just not quite yet. Besides, in my daydreams, I'd always known exactly who the father was.

Okay, except that one time I imagined Chris Evans and Chris Hemsworth fighting over me, but... that barely counted. And this was real life.

What else? Well. Some couples tried for *years* to get pregnant, even when they badly wanted it. You had to have sex at the right time in your cycle. Had to be fertile. A whole host of other things that I couldn't remember. I remembered my friend Natalie trying a whole load of crazy superfood shakes to try and coax her body into a more fertile state.

I hadn't done any of that. I'd been stupid, and let my desires run away with me without thinking about where it might lead. Surely, I could be forgiven for that. Surely the universe wouldn't...

I swallowed, and a pit formed in my stomach.

A line was fading into view — unmistakably, even when I blinked rapidly to dismiss any tricks my eyes were playing on me and pulled it closer to examine it.

I was pregnant.

My lip trembled. Moments later, I was curling over the edge of the toilet bowl retching. Fear clenched my stomach so tight I couldn't hold it. I was assailed with a train of frantic, accelerating thoughts. The impossible pain of childbirth, which I had always feared I'd never be ready to bear. The panic of having to identify the father. The thought of being abandoned; the thought of *not* being abandoned, and breaking up this family in the process.

I didn't know what to do with myself. When I finished vomiting, I slumped to the floor, head tipped back against the cool porcelain tiles, and dabbed the tears out from under my eyes with a shaking hand.

I should have expected this. Doctor Gray had a knowing look in her eyes as soon as I falteringly answered her question. Clearly, it matched all my 'symptoms'. No wonder I'd been feeling especially morose about my situation with the

North men recently. Some subconscious part of me knew exactly what I was walking into.

I closed my eyes and took a deep breath — then quickly concluded that it wasn't deep *enough*. A problem like this needed cool, fresh air. Not *technically* what the doctor ordered, but... well. The vitamin supplements wouldn't be arriving for a while. I just had to make sure that Preston and Hale didn't see me. Right now, I figured I'd break down the second any of them looked at me — let alone spoke to me or insisted I needed an escort outside. I couldn't bear sharing the truth with them just yet.

Hell. I could hardly bear it myself.

I swallowed, forcing myself to calm down for the few moments it would take me to sneak out of the cabin. Maybe this was one more stupid idea in a series of stupid ideas, but being trapped in this room with my thoughts wasn't going to help me either.

I listened at the door. There were no footsteps in the hallway. If I strained my ears, I could hear the shower running in the boys' room. My ears blushed deep red, plunging me into a graphic memory of what Hale and I had done together in there. Why did it still turn me on, even now? Even after I knew what was happening to me? Ignoring my rapid heartbeat, I closed my eyes and tried to focus. Okay, so one of them was in the shower. And the other?

Right on cue, I heard the sound of the TV buzzing into life. I couldn't make out the words, but it sounded like a newscaster's voice. Hopefully, that'd keep Hale-or-Preston sufficiently distracted while I made my escape. At least they wouldn't be expecting this. If they were, I wouldn't stand a chance of getting by them.

I stowed the test away in the bathroom cabinet, not wanting anybody to walk in on it by accident. Tying my hair up into a quick topknot, I slipped out into the empty corridor. The shower was running, and the TV still blaring. With my footsteps light, it wasn't too difficult to make my way to the back door and quietly unlatch it. Only when I was outside did I let out my breath, but the next breath in was exactly as calming and restorative as I had hoped. With the sun beaming down on me and that breeze lifting the loose strands of my hair, I felt like I might be able to handle this. At least, I'd find a way.

After all, I did have one lucky factor I hadn't considered yet. Every single one of the North men would make an excellent father. Blake's stern strength and quiet kindness would help keep any unruly child on the right path. By contrast, it wasn't hard to picture Hale pitching up the world's biggest and coolest pillow fort — or Stone reading a nightly bedtime story, complete with enthusiastic character voices and sound effects. Preston's thoughtfulness and individuality would set a perfect example for a child to follow their own path, and be mindful of their choices.

My heart throbbed. At the center of all this, no matter how much I panicked or paced, was a new life. Already, I knew that the options of terminating the pregnancy or giving the baby up for adoption were completely out of the question. Though I'd only just learned it existed, I already felt a deep connection between us which I had no intention of severing.

I just wondered which other connections I'd be severing in the process.

I looked over my shoulder as I reached the woods, wanting to make sure I kept the cabin in sight. I didn't want to go out far. After all, I knew what we were here for. Occasionally I still had startling moments in otherwise pleasant dreams when armed men broke into the cabin to hurt us. Even the memory of it was intense enough that I lifted my hand to my stomach, feeling instinctively protective.

My stomach flipped. This wasn't necessarily a bad thing, but it was scary to know that my entire life would now be pivoting to something new — that part of my old identity would fade away to be replaced by a whole new name; *Mom.*

Wait. What was that?

I froze, hearing a rustling in the trees. It sounded too heavy and deliberate and *focused* to belong to the breeze, but now that I had stopped in my tracks, the only sound I could hear was the birdsong around me. Then, a beat later, a fluttering as those birds took off into the afternoon air.

Silence again. I could practically hear my heart beating. Just as I had convinced myself that I was hearing things, I heard a branch snap a couple of meters away. As my head whipped around to identify the source, I felt movement behind me — but when I tried to scream, it was too late. A gloved hand had already clamped down hard over my mouth, dragging me backward into the bushes and much, much further away from the cabin and the North men than I had ever hoped to be.

Alarm bells started ringing the moment she didn't answer a knock on her door. No matter how down or unwell she had been over the past few weeks, Jessica had never been unresponsive — never hidden away from us. We hoped that she had just fallen asleep, but she had been a pretty light sleeper before.

I frowned, poised in front of her door. Down the hallway, a group of three uneasy North men looked back at me. The tension had been sharp enough when we had just decided to tell her the truth this evening; now, this silence behind the door was more than we were equipped for.

"Should we go in?" Preston suggested. "Is that invasive? Shit."

I knocked again, a little louder this time. "Jessica. Are you okay in there? We're worried about you."

When she didn't answer this time, I decided it was time. I glanced at Hale to be sure, waiting for his approving nod before I tried to open the door. It swayed open with almost no pressure at all — and showed us an entirely empty room behind it.

Stone didn't wait a second to start looking around the cabin. "Jess?"

"She said she was going for a nap," insisted Preston. "I swear that's what she said."

"She couldn't have gone far," I said, comforting myself as much as him. It was true, after all. She didn't have a vehicle or shifter speed; if she *had* left the cabin, it was impossible for her to be out of our range. She wouldn't be unsafe for long — not on our watch.

Now it just remained to be seen why she'd left in the first place. Frankly, that almost concerned me more than the fact of her absence. Whatever had been off about her for the past few weeks had either gotten badly worse, or morphed into something much more dangerous. Should we have revealed the truth to her sooner? I wasn't sure. I still wasn't convinced that it would make things better and not worse, but we had to try.

"Scent outside," Stone called. Without waiting, we all followed him outside. I could feel a sense of dread mounting between all four of us — not least because Jessica's scent wasn't the only one we detected on the wind.

"Alright," I said. "Stating the obvious, but spread out. Find a trace. We follow as soon as we've got a firm direction. Use whichever form is most suited; this is no time to be shy about it."

"Just don't scare her," Stone pointed out, and I nodded my approval.

"Right. Four lions sprinting at her full speed is not going to help the situation, so let's bear that in mind. Otherwise, just stay in contact. We've trained for worse."

There was no time to waste on a long monologue, and we all knew it. As much as we'd like to believe Jessica was some-where safe out here, the reality was that there *was* no safe place in these woods. Over the days and weeks, the traces of their overconfident brethren's corpses had stopped scaring them so much. While they hadn't tried attacking the cabin again just yet, they seemed to sense we were getting close. Seemed to be circling in to try and intimidate us.

It would be easy for Jessica to walk too far from the perimeter of the cabin without realizing it. Last week, Hale had spotted them within sight of the walls, and—

"Here," Preston called. I followed the sound of his voice, shifting to whip through the dense shrubbery and old tree-stumps that peppered the ground here. As soon as we were all there, he sensed us and nodded down at some scuffed footprints in the dusty dirt. "Looks like a struggle. I'm pretty sure that's her footprint over there, leading up to it."

Is there a scent? I asked

Over here. Hale tossed his head, drawing our attention to a fresh pathway that had been hacked unceremoniously through the undergrowth. *Same iron they use for their weapons. Hint of her perfume. This is it.*

Go ahead, I directed — but the order was unnecessary. Already, all four of us knew what to do. Preston joined us in his paws, running at full speed through this hacked-up walkway through the woods. Figured that they wouldn't respect the nature around them any more than they respected human life.

Or shifter life, for that matter.

It didn't take long to realize that Hale was exactly right. The metallic tang of their weapons grew stronger at every hacked branch, and every time the breeze blew back our way, it carried a hint of Jessica with it. We were heading the right way.

We're coming, Jessica.

We slowed to a quieter pace as a group, falling back into

the thick woodlands to avoid being seen. A minute later, we heard voices. Heads lowered, the deep sandy color of our bodies kept us coolly camouflaged against the dirt and dust — blended in by shadow. We would have to be careful, but with luck they wouldn't see us until we were right up close. Until we could overtake them in a heartbeat, and make sure nothing happened to Jessica in the interim.

It was difficult to know, in the heat of the moment, whether I'd made the wrong decision in bringing her here. This clearly wasn't a safe environment, as much as we had tried to make it one for her sake. Of course, if we hadn't hired her, we may never have met her, and the thought of that alternative was a sharp stone under my paw — but I also couldn't bear the guilt of having endangered her like this. If anything had happened to her…

Hey, Hale said, pressing in. Gone was the lighthearted teasing of his usual in-mind interruptions. Now, he was all business. *You're beating yourself up. I'm not looking; I can just tell. We've got this, okay? We're going to find her.*

We have to. I tossed my head, slowing my pace as the scent got closer and closer. We had reached a part of the woods we hadn't scooped out yet, with the trees packed in close together and the floor thick with discarded leaves and needles. Visibility was low here. They'd picked a good spot.

Alright — standard formation. Ears open. You all know the drill.

At my command, the four of us fell into our places like the well-practiced unit we were, neatly diverging off in our separate directions without the need to hesitate or ask questions. Most of the time, this made our paramilitary work a lot easier. Right now? It just might save our One Mate's life.

We heard their voices as background humming at first — sharp arhythmic buzzing that sounded like nothing in particular. As we got close enough to make out individual words, the pitch changed. Another voice.

Her voice.

Easy, I said, warning myself as much as the rest of them. *Hold formation. Don't rush in.*

I can see a campfire, said Preston. *Surrounded by a thicket of trees. Pretty large fire.*

Space for... what? Ten men? I asked.

No, many more. This could be their main encampment.

Stone flashed in with agreement. *Agreed. I'm beginning to see defences. Palisade walls. Preston's right; this is their base.*

If they were correct, then this was a fight we weren't properly prepared for. There was a reason we hadn't just run out and explored these woods quickly and without care; we had to be methodical and well-informed so that we could stand on the best possible footing for the inevitable fight. Right now, their decision to take Jessica had backed us into a corner. We only had half of the picture here, and the limited amount of equipment we had brought with us when we ran out.

We were going to have to think on our paws, but we had no other choice.

Anyone hazard a guess as to which side they're keeping her? I asked.

We fell into each other's minds, quickly comparing the clues we all had. With our information shared, we knew that her voice was loudest for Hale — that they must be keeping her on the far side of the encampment.

I'll close in on this side, he confirmed. *Follow in.*

Copy. We'll move in closer. Just keep your distance, I reminded them all. *We don't have the firepower to back us up if this goes south. Got to even the playing field first.*

Most of the time, working jobs like these was just second nature to us. We dealt with some of the most dangerous and amoral individuals the government could send us to meet, so engaging the enemy was never a moral hardship. Right now, though? I could feel that all four of us had hearts pumping full of angry, protective mate's blood — that the hate we felt for these assholes, whatever their number, had somehow intensified. They were extremists putting the country at risk, yes, but those crimes felt somewhat distant right now. It was secondary to the fact that they had put Jessica in danger. Treated her like some kind of bait or prize.

I hear her, Hale said. *Listen.*

We all shifted our minds to share his headspace, quickly latching onto the frantic sound of Jessica's voice.

"I swear, I don't know!"

"Don't fuck around with me, girl." This voice belonged to an older man — hard and gravelly, and as southern as they come. "If you've been living there, you know something about 'em. Let's start off simple. You know their names."

"I don't!" she insisted. "That was always part of the job. No names. No *codenames.* Total discretion. I swear, I don't know anything!"

I felt my lion's powerful muscles tighten, tense at the sound of her desperation and bravery. We knew she was made of tough stuff, of course, but to hear her fight to protect our identity like that, even in great danger, was stirring. Even if a big part of me wished she'd just come out with the truth to protect herself.

Soon enough, these bastards wouldn't be alive to repeat our names anyway.

A beat later, I had to abandon the train of thought to focus elsewhere. As the interrogation continued, I heard a quiet disturbance of the leaves ahead of me. A sentry — off-guard and unaware for now, but he wouldn't be for long.

I've got guards, said Stone.

One here too, I confirmed. *Take it easy, everyone. Take them out quiet, but only if they get too close. We don't want chaos just yet.*

Still, no matter what I said, it felt like chaos was close at hand. I could feel that familiar spark of adrenaline in my veins, edging me on towards the oblivious armed guard.

They'd taken her away from us. Now, they'd see what we could take in return.

Now that I could hear her voice, I could feel anger rippling closer and closer to my surface. Before long, I wouldn't be able to control myself. Even now, only Blake's authority over me prevented the thread from snapping. I wanted to run into that place and tear them limb from limb — any of them that had touched her or tried to scare her.

Blake knew what he was talking about, though — and he was right. If we just stormed in there all guns blazing, we'd be outnumbered and outgunned and outmaneuvered within moments. We had to wait until they were off-guard; we had to separate them and pick them off in small numbers. In other words, this wasn't the time to let our emotions get the best of us.

I paused as one of the guards drew near. He still had no idea I was there; his weapon was slung over his shoulder as though he had never even thought about having to use it, and his thoughts seemed to be occupied elsewhere. He seemed innocent enough — but he was old enough to know better than to fight for an ideology like this.

I part-shifted back to human form, retaining only the sharp claws of my left hand. Silently approaching from behind the cover of a tree, I slipped up behind him and slit his throat.

One down.

Mine's approaching, said Preston. *Any minute now.*

This part, at least, was a dance we'd taken part in many times. Granted, we were usually better appraised of what lay inside the encampment walls and how we'd deal with it once we got there — but right now, the process was the same. It felt like muscle memory at this point, barely worth thinking through.

That left a lot of space for my mind to run wild, thinking of all the terrible ways they might treat her in pursuit of information. I cared about Jess from the moment we met, but ever since we slept together, it had stacked up to something much more intense. It was as though that act of love had confirmed every suspicion, I had about who she was, and what we could be together. It felt like we'd been together for decades in those few short moments.

I gritted my teeth, covering the body of the guard in case another should come by. We were here for her now. Maybe she didn't know it yet, but the ordeal was coming to an end.

Guard out on my side, said Blake. *Hale?*

Clear for me.

And here, Preston added.

Alright, said Blake. *Move in closer for observation and bunker down. We'll wait until nightfall, unless she's in imminent danger.*

I'd follow my alpha's orders, of course, but the thought of waiting just within her reach for hours as darkness fell, hurt me. I couldn't imagine how frightened she must be down there, trying to hold up the front that she didn't know what they were asking her. Every now and again they came back to the spot they were keeping her, and they'd try again —

pushing and pressing in various different ways to try and get her to talk.

So far, they hadn't touched her. For their own sake, they'd better hope it stayed that way.

~

Once night had finally fallen, the glow from the campfire was the only thing to illuminate our surroundings. It cast long, flickering finger-like shadows through the trees and the palisade walls. Eerie-looking, but shadows had always been our friends. Tonight was no different. As the night sentry finally took over, I stirred from my position in the tree. It was nearly time. I could feel it in my joints, watching the casual arrogance of those nighttime guards — expecting nothing, and prepared for nothing.

Human form, said Blake. *Arm up and shoot to kill. We don't have the intel or the backup to handle this situation if things turn out bad. Everybody prepared?*

I felt our collective readiness. It filled up my limbs like electricity as I shifted back into human form, stretching my shoulders and my arms. A moment later, I had my pistol in hand. Heart pounding, I waited for the signal to come.

It felt like a lifetime before Blake finally said those words.

Alright. Move in.

Our movements sometimes felt like an out-of-body experience. We trained so carefully that when it came to performing a task, all of our physical movements were second nature, and we could dedicate the bulk of our thinking to strategy. As such, when I reached the thinning lines of the trees outside the encampment, it felt almost like I was watching myself — distant, somehow. When I reached the guard on the gate, there was no fear to prickle at the base of my spine. Nothing but the cool understanding of what I had to do — and the hot, raw anger that motivated all of us.

After a split second of action, the first guard was down. To my right, I saw Preston flooring another on the other side. At the front of the encampment, where the palisades parted, Hale and Blake would be closing in.

Preston ran up beside me in his human form as the first shots rang out. It took only a mere glance between us to agree, and we moved forward in unison — stepping carefully and quietly over to the now-unoccupied guards' gate. Now that the firefight had begun, this could turn into a numbers game fast. It would be our job to keep the others from being swarmed, ideally before the enemy realized we were inside.

They had certainly noticed Blake and Hale. Shouts rose up around us as we ducked behind a tarpaulin, picking off a couple of stragglers from the edges of the pack. After all this time they spent evading us, I'd expected them to be more organized than this. Sometime since they settled here, they must've grown complacent.

Any survivors wouldn't make that mistake again.

However, all thoughts of the foot soldiers around us soon evaporated as our eyes fell on a cage of wooden pikes. Half-shrouded by a tarpaulin, it lay close enough to the campfire to illuminate its sole occupant.

I took hold of Preston, his wrist tight in my hand. The urgency must have spoken to him; his gaze followed mine, and we both stood for a moment in silence as we recognized the huddled form of our mate inside this cage.

We didn't waste another moment. After a quick check to make sure we wouldn't draw attention, we slipped across the encampment square and reached her side. Our footsteps were light on the approach, but she still raised her eyes as we came near — first afraid and tired, and then wet with relief.

I lifted a finger to my lips as she made to speak, shaking my head.

Don't speak. You're okay, but we need to get you out of here.

Of course, she couldn't hear me like Preston could, but I hoped the meaning came across to her somehow. As the firelight reflected in her eyes, brow furrowed and jaw firm against the fresh onslaught of tears, I saw something braver and sturdier appear.

I squeezed her hand through the wooden bars, only retreating to help Preston as he discovered the door. Our first attempt to spring the lock was quickly foiled; instead, after a glance at each other, we realized what plan B had to be.

You ready for gunfire on our side? Preston asked. *We need to spring Jess out.*

She's safe? Blake asked. I felt Hale's mind hovering right over us, eager for the answer.

Frightened but seems unharmed, I answered. *She'll be better once she's out of here.*

There was a short period of silence, and rapid fire from the other side of the camp. Jess' hands tightened on the bars, and I was reminded that she still didn't really know what the hell was going on. That the others were safe.

I gave her a smile, instinctive and reassuring.

Do you need me? I asked, eyes still skimming over Jess as Preston continued to work the lock. *I could take her back, out of the way.*

There was a short silence as Blake weighed it up. *Take her. Preston — see them off, then come to us. Yes?*

I nodded, feeling my fellow Norths' affirmations flood my system too. There we were in sync. I put my fingers on Jess' torch gentle but serious. When her eyes met mine, I gestured at her to stand back. Mimed shooting the lock.

She nodded and pressed back against the wall. There

wasn't much space for her to move to, and she seemed to sense that — lifting her arms to cover against the upcoming blast. I stepped back, nodding at Preston.

We're ready, I thought.

Hold, said Blake. A few beats stretched out, birdsong a soft contrast against the sounds of fighting at the front of the camp. It was almost peaceful.

Of course, a second later, the pressure popped as Blake's order came through, loud and clear.

Go. Shoot.

Preston wasted no time, firing carefully to part the lock from the door. He unhooked the metal from the door and swung it open, waving Jess through as I held my arm out to shield her.

"Stone…"

I shook my head, listening out. The encampment had definitely noticed that some of the shooting was behind them; we didn't have a big window to move in.

"Follow me," I said. My voice was as soft as I could make it, but it still felt alarmingly loud compared to the silence of my usual communications in these situations. Like every armed man in these woods could hear us. "You can run?"

She nodded. That determination flashed in her eyes, and a good swathe of my fear melted away. What had I ever been afraid of? Jess wasn't some glass maiden who'd snap at the first opportunity. I'd never met a real woman who was — but her mettle right now, and her refusal to answer their questions, proved that she could take care of herself.

Of course, our One Mate would be brave like this. Nothing else would make sense.

I led her quickly back into the guards' entrance, weaving through the palisades with purpose and nimble feet. Unfortunately, my desperation to keep her safe had me distracted, and I was surprised as we came face-to-face with another guard running up from the woods."

My instinct was to play stealth and go for his neck with a clawed hand, but the last thing Jess needed was more confusion and stress right now. That left me only the nuclear option — but my moment of hesitation had cost me. The guard brought down the heavy butt of his shotgun, aiming for my head. I ducked just in time to take the blow on my shoulder instead, groaning under the weight of the impact. So long as he was hitting me and not Jess, it would be alright — but I didn't plan on giving him a second chance. Though my shooting shoulder was on fire from the hit, I lifted and sank a clean two bullets into his chest.

"Oh my God."

I came right back to Jess' side, eager to soothe away her fear. I wanted her well and comfortable, as always — but our silence was extremely valuable right now. We couldn't risk being heard now and bringing down the weight of the main fight onto ourselves.

"It's okay," I said, low and sincere. "We're alright. We just need to stay out of sight. Once we're far enough away, we'll run. I'll get you back safe, and they're going to be just fine here. Okay?"

"You're sure they're safe?"

That her first instinct was to be interested in their safety instead of her own spoke volumes — about her character, and about what we meant to her. I swallowed, wishing I could transfer to her all my care and adoration as easily as I could communicate with my pride.

For now, I could only squeeze her hand.

"I promise," I said. "They can handle themselves. Let's just get you out of here. Ready to move?"

We moved back through the trees, arching around to

steer clear of the camp's view. Eventually the sounds of the fight lay somewhere behind us, and even that seemed faint.

"Jess," I said, leading her back onto the main path. "Time to run."

Her face was steel as we ran together. She must have been exhausted after the way she'd spent her day, and after already feeling unwell, but if so then it wasn't written on her face. When we occasionally slowed to let her body rest, only then did I see the signs of tiredness — the heaviness of her breath as she bent over to recuperate her energy, and the self-deprecating smile.

"This definitely wasn't in the job description."

I grinned, leaning against a nearby tree. "Yeah, sorry about that. Should've read the small print."

"I'd have spent more time on the treadmill if I knew."

We smiled at one another, somehow finding a moment in the panic and the threat. Still, I felt that this wind of hers was mostly adrenaline — that once she was back in the safety and security of our cabin, she would process the danger she had been in, and retreat into herself a little.

It had happened to me, too, the first time. There was no way to prepare for it. I just wished it was a lesson she didn't need to learn.

"Alright," I said. "Last leg. Let's get you back inside."

"And get you patched up," she insisted. Yet again, she wasn't her own primary concern. Relief and affection filtered through me, feeling certain once again that we'd have more time together. That she'd know the truth, and be herself again.

Stone, Blake stepped in. I could feel his stamina was low. *Is she okay?*

She'll be fine, I said. *Just a little shaken.*

I could only hope that I was telling the truth.

As the light slowly faded in and chased the darkness away, marking my night from hell officially over, I felt like I was waking from a particularly vibrant dream. If not for Stone's steadying presence beside me on the couch and the silence in the rest of the cabin, I might have believed it too. The last few hours had gone by in a blur, barely strung together in my memory. How long had it been exactly? Only the lightening sky could say — but at last, Stone sat up straighter in the chair, lips pursed.

"They're coming home."

I was tired enough not to question how he knew that. It took me by surprise when I sank down into the couch just how little energy I had left; even trying to stand had made me dizzy, so Stone had been fussing over me ever since. He'd brought a blanket to wrap over my shoulders, and tea to drink; his hand seemed to find its way to mine whenever I most needed it, whether I said so or not.

By the time the door opened, it was like I'd almost run out of oxygen. My breathing was shallow and sad, and as much as I was glad to have Stone here with me, I couldn't relax until I knew that the rest of them were safe — until that door opened and all three came through, battered and bruised but *alive*.

My legs failed me again, but as it turned out, I didn't need them. They all came right to my side, and in a heartbeat, I was wrapped in all four of them — Stone's hand in mine, Hale curling down over the back of the couch to hold me, and Blake and Preston crouching at my front. Preston's forehead nestled against my knee; the whole thing, being in contact with all four of them at once, felt overwhelmingly intimate, even in the silence.

It only made the guilt in my stomach swirl all the worse. Which of these men would I hurt, once I told the truth?

"I'm sorry," I managed, after a few beats. My voice sounded raw and broken as the tears finally saw their opportunity to break free. "I didn't know that was going to happen. I just needed some air; I just—"

"You have nothing to be sorry for," said Blake. His calm voice was exactly what I needed right now, and I closed my eyes to sink into the comforting tone of it. I felt his thumb brushing the back of my free hand, and the feather-light touch of his fingertips against my wrist. "You didn't ask for that. I just wish we could've gotten to you sooner."

"I'm okay," I insisted. "I'm out."

"Technically, you did us a favor," said Hale. "We're done with this mission a whole lot earlier than we expected to be."

"You weren't ready."

"Turns out we were ready enough," said Stone, squeezing my hand again. I opened my eyes to meet his, feeling a connection course through from his being to mine. The affection and fondness I felt for all these men was almost supernatural; it made the thought of losing it and harming them even worse.

All at once, it swelled to a knot in my throat.

"I'm so sorry."

I felt a rush of kindness from each of them — a massaging grip, or a tender touch. I had lost track of whose hands were where now; instead, we all felt like one larger consciousness, melted together. Fated.

"You're safe now," Stone insisted, shifting closer to reassure me. "We're here."

I didn't know how to tell them the truth, but to keep it from them any longer would be a lie — and I certainly couldn't lie to them.

"It's not that," I managed eventually, speaking past the cracks in my voice. "I mean… it was awful, and I'm exhausted, and I'm so glad we're all here, but there's… there's something else. It's not just that."

I could feel them moving around me, and opened my eyes to see a knowing, wordless glance pass between them. I could feel my jaw tightening and shuddering as I pressed myself to speak again.

"You seem nervous," said Hale, voice a pleasant hum beside my ear. "You don't have to be."

"But it's just… what I have to tell you…"

"We already know."

I looked sideways, tugged as if strung by Stone's simple announcement.

My jaw dropped open a little, and I turned between all four of them. Brow creased and heart hammering, I tried to grapple with the truth of that. How could they know? I'd only just found out myself. Even if yesterday evening felt like a long time ago now, it was really only a couple of hours. Unless they'd gone searching thoroughly through my room, they shouldn't know — and I couldn't imagine any of these respectful, kind men doing *that*, not even while I was missing.

"Jess, it's okay," said Blake. "Let's just put that out there right away. We're not mad; we're not hurt. We're not jealous. We tell each other everything."

I tried to process what he was saying to me. They weren't *jealous*? That wasn't something you'd say about a pregnancy. So what exactly where they talking about?

My brow furrowed, and Blake found my eyes as he pressed on.

"I think there are a couple of things we ought to tell you, too."

This was not the ideal way for us to have this conversation, but we had no other option. After all our concern about her physical health, it seemed that maybe pure guilt had been harming her the whole time. It hurt to know that she'd been unkind to herself about this — that we could have alleviated the pain at any time with a dose of truth, if only we'd known about it.

Well. Better late than never.

Her eyes slipped from each of us to the next, trying to read the situation. I moved around from behind the couch to sit next to her, leaving room for Preston and Blake.

"You thought something bad was happening, being with the four of us?" I suggested.

She nodded, eyes cast down.

"You felt drawn in and you couldn't help it, even though it doesn't make sense? Like you need us just as bad as we need you?"

She turned to face me. Eyes creased with confusion and surprise, her eyes bored into mine, lips thin and unsure. "Yeah," she admitted, in a half-whisper. "Exactly that."

"Well," I said. "We're the same, Jess. Pulled to you. Wanting you."

"Since the start?"

I glanced at Stone, passing the baton to him.

"We weren't looking for someone to make us feel like this," he said. "If that's what you're asking. We really did need your help. It just happened that we met you, and… yeah, for me? I felt that right from the start."

Their eyes locked. Hearing Stone speak his truth, specifically and openly, made me feel a twist of approval and happiness in my stomach. He was an asset to our pride, much as we liked to tease each other. In this moment, I couldn't have respected him more. I could see the weight he was lifting away from Jess' shoulders, bit by bit.

"And you always knew?" she pressed, voice still stumbling. "About… when… I spent time with each of you? You're not mad?"

"No," Preston confirmed. "Not at all. We knew, and we never minded. It's not supposed to be that way between us."

"Meant to be…?"

This was a lot for anybody to take in, but I was impressed with how Jess was handling it. Though I could see a storm of questions in her eyes, she wasn't freaking out. She wasn't falling to pieces. She was just holding on for more understanding, eager to understand.

"We mean that literally," Blake clarified. "See, this is part of what we wanted to tell you, Jessica. I'm sorry we couldn't before, but… I'm sure you'll understand why it had to be a secret."

She blinked. She took a deep breath, and Blake took the opportunity to carry on.

"We are shifters," he said, in as plain a tone as he could manage. "Lion shifters."

Now it was our turn to inhale. I looked away, sure she

would prefer not to spend these few seconds being stared at. It was a lot to come to terms with, even without four pairs of eyes on you.

"Wait," she said, after a pause. "What?"

"That's why we're here," Blake continued, even and steady. "That's the special something we have that no other group can provide."

"But they're not real."

Stone rubbed the back of her hand with his thumb, drawing a gentle circle around her knuckle. "To most of the world, yeah. We know how it sounds."

"You're teasing me."

She didn't sound convinced. Clearly, this was already a lot for her to work with. To save her the mental gymnastics of trying to decide whether this really *was* an elaborate joke on her, I shuffled forward in the chair.

"Would it help to get this part out of the way if I showed you?"

Jess nodded, eyes wide. The corner of her mouth turned up in a sweet smile — half challenge, half apology.

"Alright," I said. "Let's see."

I rolled my shoulders back, already feeling the lion in me unfurl. Knowing that I was about to shift was always a thrill, even after 27 years; it was a formative but secret part of me. I had to be careful of guarding the secret, and hiding away a part of yourself didn't come naturally to anybody. It warmed me to know that Jess was finally about to see all of me — not just the human-filtered side I had been forced to limit her to.

As I slipped forward into my paws, I heard an audible gasp from Jess. When I lifted my head, great mane flopping around my face, I saw the awe on her face. To my relief, it definitely outweighed the fear.

"I..."

The others gave her a little space as she shrank to the

floor to reach out for me, one shuddering hand slowly closing the gap between her fingertips and the top of my head. Just before she reached me, I bumped my head up playfully to touch her first. She jumped, but gave a breathless laugh a second later.

"So it is you in there, huh?"

"Nothing ever changes with that one," Stone agreed. She looked between us, peering into my dark lion's eyes, and Stone's human pair.

"I don't want to be a jerk," she said, voice still sounding a little shaky, "but this is *really* weird."

I laughed, a rippling roar-purr that transformed into a sound she'd find much more recognizable as I shifted back. "Yeah, I guess it must be."

"And there you are again."

Her eyes met mine, alight with what looked like attraction. I imagined her hands on me, and watched both her smile and her blush spread.

"So it's real," she accepted, sitting back in the chair again. "And you're a... a pack?"

"A pride," said Preston. "But yes."

"It finally makes sense." Her head fell back against the couch cushion as she processed the news, though her body language was a lot more relaxed now. She seemed to be safe and secure, surrounded by all four of us. It seemed like a natural place for her to be. "And you're really not mad about...?"

"We don't get jealous about this stuff," said Stone. "Not under, uh. Certain specific circumstances."

She blinked, shaking her head. "What do you mean?"

We all turned to Blake, even Jess was able to sense the potency of his authority in this moment. When he looked at her, his eyes warmed and creased at the corners — a rare visible sign of happiness in his serious, ageless face.

"We think you're something special to us, Jessica. We think you're our One Mate."

Jess' brow furrowed in confusion, lips pursed into a tight line. I cleared my throat and answered the unspoken question. After all, this was all very new to her; she shouldn't have to ask.

"It means you're the fated partner for all four of us," I explained. "Mate to the whole pride." I traced my fingertips across her upper arm, and down over the curve of her elbow. It felt like a new level of intimacy, somehow more than the private moments we'd already shared together. She felt vulnerable and light, her skin was satin-soft. Still, the enormity of the announcement had shaken her. For a few moments, she just blinked down at her hands, thinking — then looked up, voice low.

"So. This shifter thing. It's genetic…?"

Blake nodded, but for some reason this was a tipping point for her. She closed her eyes, head falling back against the couch again. It seemed involuntary; she had gone limp.

"Jess?" Stone said, squeezing her hand. "Are you okay?"

"Lion baby," she said. "I'm having a lion baby."

JESSICA

I hadn't *fainted*. At least, I didn't think so; I could still hear all their voices around me. I was just a little overwhelmed, and had to take a moment to withdraw. Surely anybody would feel the same way? Even so, I felt an irritating flicker of weakness coursing through me. I was surrounded by these form-shifting beings, skilled and talented enough to conduct top-level government work — and here I was fading away like some damsel in distress.

Granted, I was supporting another life now, but... jeez. The kid couldn't take up that many resources so quickly, could they?

When I opened my eyes, I saw four concerned faces around me, and reddened with embarrassment. "I'm sorry," I said. "I didn't mean to freak out like that."

"Don't apologize," said Stone. "It's a lot to take in. But, uh. You said...?"

I ran my tongue over the back of my teeth. Me and my big mouth. "I said, um, Lion baby."

It was Stone's reaction that reassured me. The instant it

123

came out of my mouth, still hesitant and unsure, his eyes illuminated.

"Are you sure?" he pressed, lifting his hand to grip my forearm instead. He seemed consumed with excitement — filled to the brim with the exact opposite of the disgust and anger I had been so afraid of. "I mean. You took a test? It's — definitely, yes? You're pregnant?"

I looked between Stone and the others. His face was always easier to read than anybody else's, but I could see traces and glimmers of the same excitement in their eyes too.

"Yes," I said, after a moment's hesitation. For the first time, I felt free enough to smile about this whole situation — to acknowledge my excitement and my happiness, not just the panic and upset. It felt like ages since I'd seen that test develop, but in truth it had been less than 24 hours. As they all shifted in closer to me, hands petting and smoothing at any inch of me they could reach, I felt my eyes brim with happy tears. "I'm sure."

They peppered the bare skin of my body with eager kisses, too quick and numerous to track. Blake alone sat upright, his gaze steady and soft as he met my eyes. "As though there was any doubt about who you are," he said. "As though there ever could be."

"I don't know whose baby it is," I admitted.

He shook his head. "It's *our* baby. We'll all parent it together. The biological details are… not all that important."

I swallowed, trying to push down the knot of emotion in my throat. I had experienced such extremes of emotion today that I had no stamina reserves left to use. Still I wanted more; I didn't want to spend a second away from them ever again, but we still had so much lost time to catch up on. I felt one of their hands smooth over the flat plane of my stomach, as if feeling out for the young life inside. It would be some time yet before our baby could 'talk' back.

"Is this what you were worried about?" Blake asked. "What was making you sick?"

"Actually, no. I didn't even know until Doctor Gray came. I was worried about causing a fight between you guys. I've never... I mean. Not that I spent a whole bunch of time around military units," I admitted, lips twitching into a smile. "But I've never seen a group so tight-knit. The thought of ruining that... I don't know."

Preston fingers combed through my hair, gentle and soft. I leaned into his hand, closing my eyes, and tried to let go of all the weight.

"I guess I don't need to worry about that any more."

"Definitely not," Hale confirmed. "We just want you happy and safe."

I opened my eyes, ready with a bright smile for him — but was surprised to see looks of guilt and sadness on all their faces. I blinked, looking between them all. "Wait. What's wrong?"

"The safety part," said Stone. "We failed you on that one, pretty hard."

I flushed, shaking my head. "That was my fault. I went out for a walk by myself. I should have known better than that."

"It's our job to keep you safe," Blake said. "We're glad that you are, but-"

"We're all safe now. That's all that matters," I insisted. I felt the intensity of all their eyes on me, and took the time to meet their gazes one by one. I wanted them to know that this wasn't on them — that I didn't think they'd failed me in any way. Far from it. They'd rushed ahead their mission and risked their lives just to bring me back as quickly as possible.

I caught Blake's eyes last, strong and certain. After a beat, he relented, nodding his head.

"Okay," he said. "You're right. But still, I-"

"Ah!" I reached out for his lips with my finger, playfully

tapping him into silence. I felt him smile underneath my fingertip. "Quit while you're ahead."

"Game's over, guys," said Hale, grinning at us both. "If that's how easily she controls an alpha, we're all screwed."

We laughed, but there was already a jolt of electricity in the air between us. Before it could bubble up and over, I extricated myself from the pile and stood to face them — my four North men, all gazing at me as though painlessly staring into the sun.

"I'm going to get a shower," I announced, trying to keep my voice even. "You should all clean up too, and then — then maybe we'll see."

Either I'd forgotten how to be subtle or they were highly receptive to my suggestive tone. Whichever it was, it was immediately obvious that the North men understood exactly what I meant by that. They were already scrambling up from the couch, smoothing down the cushions and practically tripping over themselves to do what they could for me. Stone's hand was already extended to try and help me up on one side, and Hale's on the other.

"Jeez," I said, grinning. "Anyone would think I'd said something exciting." They hovered at my heels all the way to my bedroom door, stopping right at the threshold as though some forcefield held them back. When I looked over my shoulder at them, the ardent hunger in their eyes sent a flush of lust over my whole body.

Just imagining their desperate hands on me, all at one time, had my heart pounding.

"Well, go on," I said, sounding shyer than I intended. "Clean up. I won't be long."

"Yes, ma'am," said Blake, turning on his heel. Hale had already taken off down the hallway, and Preston wasn't far behind. Only Stone remained behind, eyes trailing a soft and eager line over my still-clothed body as though there wasn't a stitch of clothing on me. My toes tightened in my socks, and I felt heat throbbing inside me.

"Sure you're okay?" he asked, voice both solid and soft like candlelight. "I know this is a lot to take in. We wouldn't want to rush you into it."

That warmth crept up the back of my neck, and I had to fight myself not to close the gap between us. I wanted to kiss all that hope and sweetness off his lips until there was only something dark and animal left — but right now we had to wait. All five of us did.

"You think you four pussycats could pressure me into anything I didn't want?" I teased, shedding my sweater as I sloped into the bathroom. Looking back at him one more time, I was pleased to see desire painted all over his face. "Fifteen minutes. We'll see who's feeling rushed."

By the time I closed the bathroom door behind me, my face was flushing pure red. I wasn't sure who this woman was — this cool, confident person who was taking this entire 'One Mate' thing in stride. In the moment, it all felt so natural. The way it felt to have their hands and their eyes on me made it impossible to question. Only now that I was out of the spotlight could I begin to question myself.

This couldn't really be happening. And even if it was, why had they all chosen *me*?

The hot water beat down over my aching body, washing away the stress and uncertainty of the past 24 hours. In truth, I figured I should probably sleep off the stress and fear, but I couldn't have closed my eyes and rested right now for all the money in the world. I knew that my four North men were out there waiting for me with bated breath and eager kisses for many different parts of my body.

Once I hopped out of the shower and the roar of the water left my ears, there was only deceptive silence in the cabin around me. Feeling my nerves begin to riot, I took my time lathering on moisturizing lotion and spritzing myself with perfume — teasing my hair away from my face, twisted and fastened back in the hopes that it would dry into loose waves.

When I looked back at myself in the mirror, I was stunned to see the woman standing there. What they said about pregnancy really must be true. There was a glow to my skin, so golden and light that I almost looked unfamiliar, or even magical. I saw the rise and fall of my chest, gentle and smooth as though I wasn't panicking inside. I felt *good* in a way I hadn't in a long time — empowered by the life inside me and the effect I had on the North men, and anticipating all the pleasure to come.

I took one last deep breath to steady myself, and slipped on my dark satin robe from the back of the bathroom door. Hair still damp, I made my way through my room and the corridor to the comfort of the communal space.

There, before a softly-crackling fire, the North men — my pride — had built a soft-sheeted paradise of pillows and blankets. With the couches pushed slightly aside, the space was enough to fit all of us comfortably. They stood as I approached, half-dressed and hardening just at the sight of me. I swallowed, tongue darting out to wet my lips.

"This is perfect, what you've done," I said. "It's so beautiful."

And it was. It felt like an altar to true romance, without the rose petals and the lacy underwear that Hollywood always sold us. There was only the soft cotton of the sheets that would lie beneath us — the smoothness of our skin, and the heat from our bodies intermingling with the fire. If there was a more appealing sight, I'd never seen it.

Preston was closest to me, and held out a hand for me to take. As I took it, stepping into the security and energy of this private space, I felt Blake close in behind me, his lips pressing down softly against the back of my neck — Stone smoothing my hair away with a soft touch, and Hale's fingertips skimming the simple tie of my robe.

"Can I…?"

"Yes." I tipped my head back into Blake's kiss and let Hale do what he wanted — to unpick the knot and let the satin of my robe fall apart. I heard him inhale at the sight of my bare skin beneath, and shuddered as he drew a line from my stomach to the tip of my chin. Stone was less restrained; his arm snaked around my waist, dipping underneath the robe to touch me directly.

My heart was fluttering already. My toes curled in the soft fabric of the blanket beneath us.

I felt like a goddess, brought back to my power by their hands.

Preston's hands traced a figure of eight over the inside of my leg. I sighed, parting my legs by bare instinct, and my lip trembled as I felt him climb to his knees. His hot breath fluttered against my thigh, painfully close to my sex; I spared a hand to tangle in his hair, eyes squeezed tight shut and managing to stay upright only by the grace of Blake's presence behind me — and the pressure of his hard cock.

He and Hale worked together to slip the robe down away from my body. It pooled at my feet, no longer required in the glowing heat of the room. I felt more naked than I'd ever been, but at the same time completely invulnerable. There was no safer or better place for me to be in the world. No eyes I wanted on me more than the North pride.

Preston pressed a chaste kiss to the front of my sex as he moved his attention to my other leg, drawing a moan from somewhere deep within me. Stone's hand massaged at my hip, almost kneading the pleasure out of me with his gentle but well-aimed touch. My eyes fluttered closed again, and it was now that I began to lose track of whose hands were which — of anything tethering me to the solid and serious world outside.

There was a hand between my legs, from behind — a gentle, stroking motion that explored how wet I already was, and set the fire in my stomach that Preston's quick kiss had promised. Before long those lips were back on my front, this time pointed and purposeful. Preston's tongue — at least, I assumed it was Preston — rubbed soft and careful life into my sex, flicking slowly over my clit. In time, I felt those fingers press inside me, beginning to explore the tight warmth of my body just as Blake began to rub his cock against the curve of my ass.

I may never know what exactly drew me here to live and work with these men, or why it had to be now. All I *did* know was that things were exactly as they were supposed to be.

I gave a choked cry as that mouth pressed closer to suck at my clit, back arching and leaning back into Blake's waiting arms behind me as I submitted to the wave of fast-mounting pleasure. I wasn't sure when I moved, but when I opened my eyes it seemed I had been carefully carried down to the floor — that my legs were now wrapped over Preston's shoulders as he continued to worship my pussy, and Blake's cock against the small of my back.

When I looked to the side, I found Stone's hard cock waiting for me. I looked up to meet his eyes as I took him into my mouth, relishing in the groan it teased out of him. Hale's tongue traced a circle around my nipple, spreading the shuddering pleasure I felt to entirely new parts of my body — and just as intense. It wasn't long before I came for them for the first time, toes tensing and clenching over Preston's shoulders and still rubbing eagerly at Stone with a spare hand.

Preston looked up at me once I'd bleated out my pleasure, eyes intense with desire.

"Jess, please…"

"God, yes."

I knew what he wanted, and I needed it too. I shifted forward, feeling my weight supported by Blake and Hale beside me, and let Preston guide his way inside me. Slick-wet from his kisses and my pleasure, there wasn't the faintest discomfort as I took every inch of him, sinking down into the fireball heat of his lap.

"Fuck, Preston."

I felt the others close in around us, the heat of their bodies overwhelming in an entirely pleasurable way. Blake kneaded at the small of my back, and I could feel his cock bumping up against the backs of my legs. At either side of me I had Stone and Hale, impressively hard in my hands, and soon Stone leaned in to capture my lips in a rough, eager kiss.

It wasn't just that I couldn't tell where my body ended and Preston's began. I couldn't delineate between any of the five of us. It was as though we formed one amorous creature, damp with sweat and desperate for *more, more, more.* As Stone pulled away from our kiss, I buried my face into his hair — breathed in the woody musk of his scent, still flooded with the taste of his kisses.

"Jessica." Only Blake was still solemn enough to use my full name, even as lust tinged it with urgency — made it sound like a litany more than a name. "Would it be too much, if…?"

"No," I moaned into the side of Stone's head, following the pattern of Hale's kisses over my shoulder and my neck. "Not too much. *Please.*"

He didn't need to finish the sentence for me to know what he wanted. Sure enough, Preston slowed his thrusts to give Blake a chance to press up even closer behind me, guiding himself into place. When he finally pushed inside me, I felt the searing bliss of both of their widths together, melting back against Blake's chest and losing myself in Stone and Hale's devouring kisses.

I felt that I'd been made for this. Made to carry their child — made to curl and stretch to the shape of them, heart pounding to the rhythm of all four lovers at once.

Was it too soon to call it love? I didn't think so. Every trailing touch of Stone's fingertips felt like fire; every circle Hale's tongue traced over me made me feel a little more alive than the second before. When my pleasure mounted to another powerful orgasm, my eager cries and tight clenching brought Preston to his peak inside me. In the moment, I couldn't be sure whether it was him or Blake. Only when he withdrew, leaning forward to offer a line of kisses down my body, could I draw my own conclusions. It wasn't long before Hale moved in to take his place, Preston cupping my chin to draw our lips together. The intersection of those feelings — the desperate, wild pleasure of Blake and Hale thrusting inside me together, and the sweet satisfaction of Preston's romantic kiss — was surreal and powerful.

A hand snaked down to draw tight circles around my clit, so good and unexpected that my back arched hard again. I opened my eyes to see that it was Stone's hand, fast and focused; with Preston still kissing at my neck, I reached down for Stone's cock to devote all my attention to him, carried away on a raft of bliss.

Before long, Hale was following Preston over the edge — withdrawing from me to finish neatly on my stomach. As he made to move away, my hand closed around his wrist.

"Is there lube?"

"Uh-huh. Are you uncomfortable?"

"No," I answered. As Blake hit deep inside me, I arched back against him again, punctuating my point; still, Hale returned with lubricant. I still couldn't speak from the pleasure, but he took initiative, squeezing a little into his palms to massage over my thighs.

Only when I'd gathered my breath could I speak up, lifting my head to meet Stone's eyes. "I want both."

"Like before?"

His brow furrowed, unsure — but Blake understood. He reached around me to slick up his fingers with lube, then slipped back down again to a tighter, more intimate hole.

"Like this," he murmured, his voice a gratifying hum. My head tipped back onto his shoulder as I moaned out my pleasure, feeling the exquisite stretch of his first finger inside me. Stone seemed to understand then, moving between my legs to guide me down onto his waiting cock. I still had Preston and Hale on either side of me, smoothing lube-slick hands over every free part of my body. It felt like an all-over massage, and even more so once Blake added a second finger. The white-hot intensity of feeling them fill both parts of me at once had my heart hammering and my skin tingling all over. Last night's danger had vanished from my memory, along with any thought of uncertainty or shyness or discomfort.

At last, Blake withdrew his hand and pressed his cock inside me instead. I gasped, legs tightening around Stone's body as I felt inch by tantalizing inch of Blake sink slowly deeper. He was careful and gentle — and Stone had slowed too, giving me a chance to assimilate to the new two-pronged rhythm of our love.

"God, *yes*."

I accepted eager kisses from Preston and Hale as we rode out this final stretch together, groaning against their lips and feeling more undone by the second. I could feel myself mounting to one last peak, with Stone's thrusts growing ever more urgent, and his thumb still strumming a delicious rhythm over me. Soon, I felt Blake begin to tense too;

knowing that both of them were ready to come for me, hard and eager, drove me over the precipice, and I came one last time with a desperate cry.

As Stone and Blake finished, staggered one after the other, my body remained tense between them. I felt a last lick of lust as I felt Blake's mouth on my neck — a hard, satisfying bite that tugged me back under a wave of pleasure all over again.

We lay in a floppy, fulfilled pile, limbs intertwined around one another. I felt the body heat of all four lovers pressured up close against me, desperate for as much of my skin as they could contact. They covered me with such efficacy that I barely felt naked, sighing with the weight of my pleasure underneath the cozy last traces of our sex.

"That was incredible."

I smiled at their hums of assent, and as I felt Blake's hands wind into my hair, coaxing out the tangles.

"You're perfect," he said, keeping his voice soft and low. "Exactly what we needed, even before we knew it. Before we could have hoped."

I glowed in his praise, nestling closer to the sound of his voice. The rest of the Norths moved with me, keeping me close and protected in the center of their love-pile. "You're all perfect too," I told them, and meant it. I'd never had a partner that felt so right or natural — never felt so loved or desired. The knowledge that a life of ours was growing inside me only sharpened my happiness. "I… really can't believe how lucky I am."

I felt several hands come to rest gently over my stomach, and knew they were thinking of the same bundle of joy.

How had I ever imagined this would be a *bad* thing?

"We're the lucky ones," said Hale, drumming his fingertips lightly over my skin. "Trust me. We really are."

"All five of us will be," said Stone. "When the little one comes."

"I've been thinking about names," I admitted. "Just a little." Seeing their ears perk up, I smiled and continued. "Is it too cliché to call them Leo, or Leona?"

Preston grinned. "Not for me."

"Will they actually be a shifter?" I asked, sitting up a little. I propped myself up against Blake's lap, wriggling back closer as his arms wrapped around me. "I still have so much to learn."

"More than likely, yes," Blake answered, lips resting on my shoulder where he'd bitten down. It felt a little sore now, but in a good way — a physical remnant of all their love. "Don't worry, though. You've got plenty of time to learn."

"All the time in the world," Hale confirmed.

As we lay there, drifting off in a happy pile by the glow of the fire, that was the thought I fixated on. For most of my life, I'd been wondering exactly where I'd end up, and with who — daydreaming about whether I was working the right job, or keeping the right company, or dating the right men. Now, seeing this path laid out before me, I felt a surreal calm and happiness settle over me like a blanket.

I wouldn't have to struggle or wonder any more.

STONE

Our commanding officers didn't need to know the minute detail — didn't need to hear that we'd all risked our lives, and the integrity of the mission, to rescue Jessica. As natural as it was, and as much as we'd all stand behind the choice, it went directly against protocol, and none of us much enjoyed the idea of never being allowed to work as a unit again.

Instead, we just made out that we'd stumbled across their base camp early. That we'd seized an opportunity once we had adequate intel and knew exactly what we were walking into.

If anybody at the Pentagon suspected that we'd made some early moves, they didn't say so. They just seemed grateful that the problem was handled sooner than expected, and without any casualties to the unit — or media attention. We were ghosts, slipping in and out of the area without causing any mayhem. It was exactly the reason they recruited us as a unit in the first place.

Now, of course, we could start heading home.

Still, it felt a little bittersweet to be leaving. This cabin was so much more than a workplace now. It was the place where we'd found Jess — or at least where we found our feelings for her. I knew she was special from the first moment we met and interviewed her, but learning over the course of these months exactly *how* special she was? That was a gift I'd never forget. As I walked through the communal areas of the cabin, checking for any possessions we'd left behind, I almost wished we could hold onto the place. Make it our own, for getaways.

But hey. If we had to leave it behind forever, so be it. Home is where the heart is, and we'd soon be making memories with Jess there too.

Speaking of Jess? I had an intervention to run.

"You know I'm not going to let you do that, right?"

She looked up at me from the kitchen, hand poised over the sink ready to dampen down a cloth. Her smile was playful and sheepish, as though she'd almost been expecting to get caught.

"I'm not *that* pregnant yet."

"Step away from the cleaning products, Dorsey." I closed in on her, tugging the cloth out of her hands and pressing a kiss onto her blushing cheek. "Don't make me tell Blake. He *will* make you sit out in the sun with a glass of ice water and a plate of strawberries."

"I'm considering it anyway," said Blake, stepping in from outside and brushing off his hands. "Has she been working again?" He and Hale had been loading things into the truck for a while now, and the sun had left a sheen of sweat across his forehead. I saw Jess' eyes lingering on his vein-roped forearms, and grinned.

"She's been trying," I told him. "Apparently she's 'not *that* pregnant.'"

"I'm not!" she insisted. "I'm not even showing. You're all way too sweet to me."

"No such thing," called Preston, clambering up through the basement floor with the last of our supplies. "And they're right. You're not lifting a finger."

"Are you going to let me unpack when we get home?"

"Nope," I said, cheerfully wiping down the kitchen surfaces she'd been intending to clean. "Absolutely not. We'll take care of all of that for you. And before you ask — nope, we're not going to let you pack up your old apartment either."

"If you're not careful, I'll get used to it," she warned. "Then I'll be the laziest mommy this little cub could ever have."

"I think growing an entire person is work enough," said Blake, smoothing Jess' hair behind her ears. "Anyway. Truck's loaded up. Hale's doing one last sweet of the cabin. After that, I think we're good to go."

I tossed the rag into the sink, with the countertops now clean enough to catch the sun. "Want me to call the commander?"

"Yes," said Blake. "You do that."

"I'll even let you hit dial," I teased Jess, sliding into the seat beside her on the couch. "Since you're so keen to do some work."

"Oh, screw you," she said, curling up against me. "Stop being good to me. I hate it."

I kissed the side of her head, enjoying her teasing, and dialed the number on our sat phone. It didn't take more than a couple of rings for the commander to answer.

"Unit A7."

"Yes, sir. Just wanted to update you on our position. Leaving in T-minus 15, approximately. No gear left behind."

"Inclusive of data?"

"Correct, sir."

"Good. Glad you boys are heading home. You've done good work for us out there."

"Thank you, sir." My arm tightened around Jess, squeezing her shoulder. "And our support personnel too. Couldn't have done it without her."

"Of course," he said. His tone suggested he hadn't thought of her, and still didn't really make much of her contribution — but whether the commander believed Jess was indispensable or not was kind of immaterial to the truth. However, this task had turned out, it certainly wouldn't have been as easy or as enjoyable without Jess here with us. It wouldn't have been over as quickly, either. Even now, the thought of her captured made me flutter with anger — but it also reminded me that she hadn't given them a word of information, not even when her life was in danger.

She was something special. Our commander's nonchalance was irritating, but I didn't need his confirmation to know that. I hoped she didn't either.

The drive felt so much longer on the way out to the cabin than it did on the way back. A few months ago, the North men were driving me into the unknown. I had barely known any of them, and only really felt friendly with Stone to begin with. Now, it was a completely different story. We were heading back to a civilization I knew well, and I was surrounded by company that I loved. Company that loved *me*. No matter who was driving and who slept, the time passed quickly and with laughter.

By the time I started recognizing landmarks and buildings in our home city, I was almost sad to be away from that wilderness where we'd all fallen for one another. I could only hope that our feelings would be the same out here, where they could find any number of pretty girls to occupy their time and bear their children.

Preston squeezed my hand as we pulled up to the North men's home. I barely remembered it from my interview. Now that I was arriving here with an invitation to live there, it felt like a completely different environment. I found myself taking light and cautious steps as I headed up the driveway to the front door, almost nervous of what I'd see inside. As though it wouldn't measure up to the dreams of the busy family life I'd been envisioning back at the cabin.

"Welcome home," said Stone, as he unlocked the door.

As it swung open, every fear I had melted easily away. The hallway inside already smelled like all four North men in some innate, natural way — not the aftershave they wore or their shampoo, but the core of them. A wave of comfort washed over me as we stepped inside, Blake following us in with my bag.

"Of course, you can live at your own place for as long as you like," he assured me. "There's no pressure to run on in here. We want you happy and relaxed. But… you can consider this place home just as soon as you want to."

"It already feels like home," I admitted. I ran my fingertips over the back of the couch, and imagined us all piled together in front of the fire here, just as we had in the cabin. There was a lot more space for us on this floor — and the plush, soft faux-fur rug on the floor looked like it would provide a pretty comfortable place to lie.

Everything was perfect. The only factor I couldn't guarantee was me.

I turned to face all four of them, smiling faintly.

"It's beautiful here," I said. "It really *does* feel like home. I want to be here. I just… I hope I'm not a disappointment."

Hale's brow furrowed. "How could you be?"

"I don't know." I folded my hands. "I've never been a mom before. Never had four boyfriends at once. I don't know how to do any of this. Outside of that cabin, and all that honeymoon feeling… I just don't want to let you down. That's all."

They closed in around me, and I leaned into Stone as he came close, Blake's hand fastening into mine.

"You don't need to worry about that," Blake promised.

"You're our One Mate, Jess. I'm sorry if we haven't made it clear enough, but… don't you know what that means?"

I shook my head against Stone's chest.

"It means we're fated for each other," Hale explained, his soft voice taking up the mantel for Blake. "Some part of you calls out to some part of us in a way we'll probably never fully understand, but… it's very, very strong. Doesn't matter how out of place you feel, or how new you are to this. We're all yours now. Protectors. Lovers. Fathers to your children."

I swallowed, sitting back to meet their eyes. When they'd explained this before, it certainly felt seismic — but these words right now, spoken with such sincerity in my new home, were stirring me to greater heights of emotion.

Preston smiled down at me, reaching for my other hand. "So long as you want us," he added. "So long as we can make you happy."

"You will," I assured them. "I can feel that."

"But you don't know quite how," Blake said, squeezing my hand. "You just… know it. There's just something in your center, whispering about it. Sure as the sun."

"Yeah," I agreed. That was exactly how it felt. Is that what they meant by 'fate'?

"That's what we feel too," Stone said, brushing through my hair. "So it seems like destiny made its choice about us, but… it's important to us that you're here by choice, too."

Hale nodded. "If you're not sure. If you decide you don't want this…"

"You're always free," Blake said. "You will be no matter what. But just for the avoidance of any doubt…" He lifted my hand to his lips, pressing a soft kiss to my knuckles. "Let me ask you officially, on behalf of the pride. Be our One Mate?"

Hearing the honesty and the vulnerability of those words took my breath away. Here was Blake, pride alpha with the power of four human men, with his voice soft and his heart open. I felt my eyes brimming with tears as I looked between all four of them.

Something called me to that job ad a couple of months ago. I couldn't possibly have known it was this — but was it fate pulling me towards this moment in time all along?

"Of course, I will," I managed, through the tightness in my throat. "Yes."

I could have been imagining things, but it felt like a lasso of light had tightened in around us, fastening us together for the good times and the bad. I felt overwhelmed with their love and support, and closed my eyes against the intensity of the feeling as they all pressed in around me, showering kisses on my body and holding me tight and close. Somewhere inside me, our child was growing, unaware that it had four heroes for fathers.

"I don't know how I'm going to explain it to my mom," I admitted.

Hale's laughter was infectious, spreading first to Stone and then to me. It even claimed Blake in the end, tugging a wayward smile onto those serious lips of his.

"You tell her whatever you want," said Blake. "We'll cross that bridge when we come to it. What I care about right now is making you happy here."

"We can set you up in one of the spare rooms," said Preston. "And start setting up the nursery. Never too early, right?"

I beamed, sinking down onto the arm of the couch. With them all surrounding me, it really didn't feel too soon. It felt like the manifestation of a fairytale. I just couldn't believe that this was my real life — that over the space of a few months, I had walked into this perfect ready-made family, and was about to start making decisions about nursery colors and baby names.

Only one potential thorn stuck out.

"You guys won't disappear on me every couple of weeks for another long mission, will you?" I asked. After all, that was what they did. They solved problems for the government, all as one unit, in places not safe enough for children — and it took time.

"We'll cross that bridge when it comes to it," said Blake. "If we all have to leave you alone, then no. We won't go."

"But you-"

"We exist," Hale interrupted, "to take care of you and our family. That's what we're for now. Everything else is… peripheral."

"We'll still need to pay bills," I said, only half-teasing. "And won't you get bored? My four big, strong men who fight extremism, forced to stay home with the kids."

"Forced?" said Stone, brows raised and mouth turned up in a wicked smile. "Are you kidding? It's what I've always wanted."

"And me," said Preston. "You have no idea how many times I've made mental bookmarks of things to share with my future children."

Hale shuffled back to lean against the couch, pointing at a nearby shelf. "*That* is a trophy from when I played soccer at high school, and you can bet your life I'm ready to become the most over-eager and competitive parent at my kid's practice."

I turned to Blake, feeling the power of his silence. I needn't have worried, though. His eyes were kind, and another rare smile had crept onto his face.

"If I gave up my career, it wouldn't be a day too soon," he said. "I love the military, but I've given years of my life to it. I'd be happy coming off the front line to serve some other way. To stay at home. I could strategize, for one thing. I could train up recruits."

"God help those recruits," teased Hale.

I smiled, half entertained by their back-and-forth and half relieved. Evidently, every single one of the North men had thought about this before. It was reassuring to know that this had been a dream of theirs for a while — not something that was being thrust upon them by a roll of the dice and a random speight of fertility.

Not for the first time, I felt strongly that it really didn't matter who was the biological father of the child. All four of them would be strong and loving parents. All four of them were ready to take on the task. Whatever color we painted the nursery, and however long it took us to choose a name, this child was going to be one of the luckiest ever born. How many people could say they had *two* committed parents, let alone *five*?

I stood from the couch, walking to look out of the window at the beautiful stretch of green land behind the house. I could imagine them all running out there as lions, our sweet cub trying their best to keep pace.

Maybe a couple of our cubs. Only time would tell now.

"Jessica?" Stone prompted, still standing by the couch. "Are you okay?"

I smiled, leaning on the windowsill. I drew in a deep breath, absorbing the scent of home. Then I turned around, a warm and eager smile on my face.

"Here, with the four of you? More than you could ever know."

Keep reading for a sneak peek of the next book!

TAMING HER BEARS

The whipping helicopter blades overrode the sound of the wind lashing the ocean into a fury as it circled around so close to the chopping water, it splattered up over the landing skids.

"Time to get your feet wet, seaman," yelled Darkhorse in my ear.

I crossed my arms over the inflatable life-saver, squatted at the door, and turned a somersault into the ocean below. Even through my insulated suit, I could feel the water's chill. I gasped as I came up for air, my nose red and cold. The released tube inflated automatically.

The fisherman had been treading water but was starting to panic. He'd been too long in the ocean, had swallowed too much of the salty surf that washed up over him. He saw the life-saving tube and began waving his arms up and down, drowning himself. I caught him in a half-nelson, from behind, hauling him toward the tube. Within seconds, the helicopter was hovering directly overhead, dangling a harness and ropes.

The fisherman clung to the tube, his mouth wide open

and gasping for breath, water streaming from between his lips. I wrapped the harness around him, buckled him in, and gave a thumbs up to Darkhorse before I started looking around for other survivors. Roy was harnessing in a fisherman who was barely conscious. Blood gathered around an abrasion on his head. I saw one other survivor clinging to a plank and swam over to him, shouting over the roar of the storm and the helicopter's blades, "How many were in your boat?"

I had to repeat myself before he caught it. "Four," he shouted back.

Four. Shit. I scanned the wreckage area, trying to locate another body. Nothing. They weren't more than a half-mile from shore, though. If the fourth man was a good swimmer, it was possible he had reached land. However, the weather wasn't going to make it easy to find him. Rain was pelting furiously on the ocean and steaming up a fog on the mainland. I signaled for the harness and hitched up our third fisherman.

It was a story heard often in the dark, treacherous waters where the Pacific meets the Arctic. The fishermen had been several miles from shore when the storm began moving in. They had tried to reach safety, but their skiff was buffeted with the first winds, driving it toward a treacherous underwater rock cropping. The boat ground along the edge of a sharp rock, splitting the bottom through the middle. In the storm, they hadn't been able to tell how far out to sea they were, or if there was any possibility of rescue.

"You were lucky the harbor master saw you out on the water," said Captain Josh from the pilot's seat. "He called you in."

"I hope you find Harry," said one of them miserably from under his wool blanket. "It won't be the same without him."

I put another blanket over him and handed him a cup of coffee. "You were close to shore. He could be there."

"We were wearing vests, but they got shredded up on the rocks and weren't much good anymore. Maybe Harry's came out better."

"Maybe it did. Your vests still saved you from the rocks."

You don't tell people to give up hope—not out here. Hope is the only thing that keeps everyone going. We hope for a better summer. We hope for a good hunt. We hope to survive the winter.

"I radioed for another chopper," shouted Josh toward the back. "We're taking the three of you to Valdez hospital. You need treatment for hypothermia."

They weren't well-positioned to protest. Two of them were under breathing masks. The third gentleman—the stalwart one who had clung to a piece of board and was now telling us their tragic tale—was shivering so hard, the floorboards clattered.

We had barely settled on the landing pad and delivered our fishermen to the waiting arms of the medics, and were thinking about steaks and show girls, when Captain Josh ordered us back into our seats. "Look lively, girls. They haven't found the fourth fisherman yet. We're doing a sweep of the coast."

I stifled a groan. The fickle autumn weather had left us to deal with a flurry of incidents over the past few weeks—an oil barge that had been marooned off-course, a fishing vessel that had grounded, a plane that went down near the Aleutians. The winds had a will of their own, turning and twisting and snatching things right up out of the sky. We were out on assignment more often than we were on dry shore.

"Don't worry," said Darkhorse, slapping my knee. "Cindy Moore will be there when we get back. She dances all night."

I shrugged. "She's been talking a lot of weird shit lately. She says she can't trust anyone because of Denisovich."

"Who the hell is Denisovich?"

I spread my hands, palms out. "How the fuck should I know? She can't trust me because she can't trust anyone, so she can't talk about him."

"Does she know you're Coast Guard?"

"That's just it. She doesn't trust anyone who makes a living piloting the ocean. That's just how she said it, piloting the ocean."

Darkhorse leaned back and folded his arms over his chest. "That's stark raving cuckoo."

The storm had let up enough along the coastline that the clouds were peeling back, revealing a solid wall of conifers marching up to a narrow, sandy beach. We fell quiet as we scanned the ground litter intensely, looking for a sign of the missing fisherman. We were about fifteen minutes into the sweep when Josh received a message over his headphones.

"They found him. About five miles north of here. He washed up on a shoal, unconscious but alive."

He started to turn the chopper around, but then did a wide swing. "Is that smoke?"

He was pointing at one of the nearby islands that hung like jewels in the Valdez bay. Darkhorse grabbed a pair of field binoculars and leaned out the open helicopter door, only his hand gripping the metal rail to keep him from falling. "Affirmative. That looks like smoke. We should probably get the fuck outta the way."

The captain was already starting the swing, his brow pressing into a tight furrow. "The rain would have put out the fire by now, but I want to know what caused it. That's a lot of smoke."

Captain Josh is a lunatic. The more adverse the weather, the better he likes it. We're the first responders' first respondents to the worst crises on the ocean. He swung about so sharply, Darkhorse had to pull himself in with a "whoop!" to keep from flying out the door.

"Damn, Josh," he chided. "Don't be so eager for my baptism."

The captain answered back, "Quit riding the skids like a horse."

"Can't help myself."

It was probably the truth. Darkhorse was the same way on the cutter. He would lean over the bow as far as his balance would allow and grin right into the face of old man wind. He rode the boats the way a cowboy rides his horse.

The island was primarily one dense growth of trees, with two or three seasonal shacks built close to the shore on the east side and a boat harbor to the south. The smoke was coming from the far western end. Josh eased the chopper until it was breezing just over the trees, with a clear view of the landscape below the cloud cover. There it was—a fried-out patch sitting next to a stream about a half-mile inland.

Darkhorse scanned it quickly with his binoculars. "Looks like someone's lodge burned down. Just an all-around bad luck day."

"We'll call it in," said Josh, picking up altitude and heading toward the main shore.

What happened next seemed to occur in slow motion, but felt lightning fast when thinking back to it afterward. We all heard a loud "ping" coming from the tail. Darkhorse half-stood and shouted, "What the fuck? Did we get shot at?" At the same time, Josh was fighting for control over the craft which began lurching and circling, nose to tail.

The copter tipped dangerously to its side and the ocean reared up, spinning drunkenly. We were about to do a nose-dive. "Jump!" commanded Captain Josh. "Everybody, jump."

I didn't need any more persuasion. I jumped.

NATALIA

I told Rhoda not to trust the bikers. They weren't the kind that usually hung around—road warriors on the weekends, working a nine-to-six job during the week, just using the wilderness as a playground for their bikes. There was something harder, more intense about these guys when they showed up at Pioneer Pete's, the lodge all the locals went to on the weekends to let their hair down and try again at relationships that didn't work the first time around.

Rhoda couldn't resist. The dudes had money. They had good drugs. They had kick-ass bikes that could follow a mountain goat's trail. Rhoda had short-circuit attractions when it came to men. She liked men that drove big cars and big bikes. She liked men with money. The more they flashed, the better she liked them. When the bikers asked if we wanted to take a spin, I went along, hoping to keep her out of trouble.

I cursed under my breath. I was a state trooper; I should have at least been carrying a gun. I didn't think about it at the time. I was off-duty, ready to hook up with a good-looking hunk of muscle and bone. They had all kinds in Valdez—the brawling fishermen that couldn't wait to spend their money after three months at sea; the pipeline workers with arms of steel; construction workers; fish and game. Valdez wasn't really on my beat, just a nice place to drop in on when traveling from Haines to the South Central.

What really pissed me off was that I hadn't seen this coming. I was prepared for trouble along the trail. The dudes weren't really that bad looking, they just had a way of looking narrowly at each other. They were speaking with their eyes, and it made me uneasy. My trusty Buck knife was tucked inside my boot, where it always was, and there were only two of them. I could take them both on. My dad didn't raise a wimp—he raised a ball-busting officer of the law.

But our chaperones didn't stop along the trail. They arrived at what looked like an ordinary biker's club. Several other bikes were parked in the yard, and live music was jamming inside. I thought I knew our bikers well, but apparently, they still had a few surprises for us. This spot was popular. The club was rocking like I hadn't seen since the last time I went to a Talkeetna festival.

I didn't recognize anybody there, although the girls all seemed to be from the villages. They all had that village-girl look to them: wide-eyed, overly excited, their complexions too healthy to be biker whores. That should have tipped me off, right there. The bikers always had a handful of worn-out, drug-addicted fans lurking around their clubs, willing to do anything they were asked. These girls were just innocents taking a ride in the fast lane.

I let my guard down. I mingled. I downed a couple of beers. I was beginning to enjoy myself. As a group, I've seen worse, like the fat, balding types that don't realize they no longer look twenty and the ones that forgot their toothbrushes. These guys were a little seedy, a little too cold around the edges, but the big guns were in all the right places. I started getting into the scene.

The last thing I remember was leaning against a wooden supporting beam, talking with one who seemed mildly better-looking than the others. His eyes seemed kinder, his smile more sincere. Then, I was out. Just like that.

I cursed again, struggling with the ropes. They had slipped something into my drink, just like I was a rookie. Pathetic. "We've got a lively one!" announced someone. I tried to peek through the blindfold. I knew I was on a boat. I could feel the ocean waves under me, hear the whine of the engine.

A voice answered back in Russian, then said in heavily accented English, "Take the blindfolds off. We're almost there."

Daylight streamed into my eyes and I squinted them shut. When I opened them again, I saw that we were in a large speedboat, zipping between a cluster of islands. I wasn't very familiar with the island chains. They followed the entire mainland, from the Panhandle to the Aleutians. I could be anywhere. I was sitting in the bottom of the boat, bound and gagged, with Rhoda and two other women.

"Take the rag out of their mouths, too," instructed the Russian pilot. "They can scream now. Scream all they want. Nobody will hear."

I squirmed backward as far as I could when the crewman bent over to release the gag. If only I could reach my boot, but my arms and wrists were bound too tightly. "Scream now," sneered the crewman, untying the gag. I cursed and spat in his face. He backhanded me hard enough to crack my forehead against the side of the boat.

"Not too much!" ordered the pilot. He was steering the boat toward shore, shouting over his shoulder. I saw a hand-hewn wooden pier bobbing in the water and a small fisherman's cabin. He slowed down until the engine was only a quiet mutter. In a more controlled voice, he added firmly, "No damage. We want no damage. We want perfect."

One of the girls was screaming. Rhoda and the other one were both crying in deep, despairing sobs. I blinked back tears of my own. I wasn't giving these slimeballs the satisfaction. "She thinks she's a tough girl, a real bad ass," the crewman remarked with a grin. "She'll break. They all break."

"But not for you." The pilot pulled up alongside the pier. Two men dressed much like the bikers, in leather jackets and jeans fitted tightly around the butt, came out of the cabin and rushed down to the pier to help with the tie-off. With the boat secure, the pilot picked me up and threw me over his shoulder like a sack of potatoes. "Tough girl, eh?" He made a signal with his free hand. "Let's bring them in."

There were three other girls already in the cabin, all from the party. They were also bound, hand and feet, and left discarded on the floor. The four men apparently intended to burrow in for a couple of days. A stack of firewood was piled near the door, and the pot-bellied stove in the middle of the room was crackling and pouring out heat. On top of it was a tea kettle and a pot of beans. A table in one corner was littered with junk food wrappers, fast food leftovers, and paper plates. The men wandered in and out, taking turns guarding us and eating whenever they pleased.

The pilot murmured something to the crewman, who opened a water bottle. "Anyone thirsty?"

We all were. Still hungover from the party and the effects of the drugs, we opened our mouths as obediently as baby birds. I hesitated, but the cap had been sealed. The water was clean. I let him pour it into my mouth, and it dribbled down my chin. My throat felt hot and dry. The water was soothing.

"I have to go to the bathroom," said one of the girls.

The pilot scowled but indicated with a lax hand that

someone should untie her feet and take her outside. Her guard left the door open in front of him. I scooted around to see where he was taking her. Their john was a collapsible frame and canvas porta-potty. Her guard stood in front of it until she came out, then hauled her by her elbow back to the cabin and pushed her inside. She stumbled and rolled across the floor, her feet kicking out. The guard laughed and grabbed her ankles while she squirmed helplessly.

"Oh, I'd do ya, hon. I'd do ya, but the boss says no damage." He drew her knees together and ran his hand up the soft inner thigh. "Sorry I've gotta do this. I'd rather see your legs spread wide, but this is how it goes. You're merchandise, hon. You're going to fetch a pretty penny."

He re-wrapped her ankles quickly, tightly enough for her to cry out, then chuckled and slapped her on the bottom. "It's not that bad. You might as well get used to how things are gonna be."

I glanced at the pilot who, so far, had intervened with rough play. But he only watched in amusement, clearly not at all concerned with psychological damage. We were cargo. "Anyone else like use the potty?" he asked. Despite our discomfort, we declined for as long as possible, not relishing the manhandling we would undoubtedly receive in return.

It was late in the evening when we heard the mutter of diesel engines chewing up the coastal waters, growing louder as the boat came closer. The men grew excited. They blew out the kerosene lamps and stood at the door, weapons ready. When the pilot gave the signal, they all filed out.

In the dark, I saw my chance. I rolled close to Rhoda and nuzzled at her hands. "In my boot, I have a knife. Pull it out. We'll fight our way out of here."

"I can't, Natalia." She was sobbing. "I'm afraid they'll kill us."

"Do you want to be a slave?"

"I want to live!"

I heard a series of gun shots. The girls in the room all screamed. I think I did, too. But I felt more rational as soon as I did and began listening closely. Only one volley of shots. Either someone had been taken by surprise or it had been a signal. If I was going to do something, I needed to do it now.

I couldn't get Rhoda to help, so I tried loosening the ropes on my own. I hadn't gotten very far when the men came back in. They were all stamping their feet and patting each other on the back. The pilot relit the lamps and beamed. "Your lucky day. Your ride is here."

They weren't in a hurry. They packed up gear and equipment and went over the details of their big heist, partly in English, partly in Russian. "Hey!" I shouted out. "I have to go to the bathroom."

The crewman looked at me, annoyed. "Can't it wait? There's a bathroom onboard the boat."

"No. I have to go now."

Disgusted, he threw down the pile of blankets he was holding and untied my feet. "Just hurry up, do you hear? We've got to get ahead of a gale."

He turned me around and searched my hands, then searched my boobs. I held back a grimace of disgust as his hands circled around the nipples, pinching the tips. "Go on then," he relented, pushing me forward. I went inside the canvas outhouse and pulled the curtain shut.

Squatting on the floor next to the toilet, I pulled out my knife, palming it open. I slid it under my wrists and cut through the ropes. At the back of the toilet, I sliced an L-shaped flap and peeked out. There was nobody in the woods behind the cabin. They were all at the pier, getting ready to move out. I made a long slice, sucked in my breath, and slipped out. I heard a shout and I dropped to the ground, but it wasn't about me. The captain on deck, or whoever he was, stood at the bow, ordering the men to move more quickly and get the damned girls on board. I slid backwards into the woods, eyes on the camp.

As soon as I was under cover of the trees, I began to run. I didn't have an escape plan in mind. This was an island and the only way off was by boat, but I felt if I stayed hidden long enough, they would leave, and I could somehow find a way to survive until help came. I found a tall, rugged spruce tree with lower limbs as big around as my leg. I climbed up into the branches, going as close to the top as the tree would bear without bending.

It wasn't long before I heard them pass by. Only three were searching the brush. The rest were probably guarding the girls. They passed directly under the tree. "We might as well go back. The storm is kicking up. Denisovich wants to get ahead of it."

"One more pass. If we don't find her, they'll take it out of my paycheck."

"It won't be that bad. You've got, what… six others in the bag? That's a lot of juicy fruit, my king."

"One more pass." They spread out, looped around, and met back under the tree.

They heard the long boat's whistle. "We'd better go, dude."

"And the girl?"

"She can't go anywhere. We'll burn the place down. Nobody will notice in the rain. We'll send out a skiff to pick her up when the storm is over. She'll either be dead by then, or she'll be dead when we're through with her."

Warlock's Claim

Historical Paranormal Romance

Secrets of Storyville

A Countess Betrayed

A Harlot Betrothed

Epic World Building Academy Romance

The Broken Academy

Power of Fire

Power of Magic

Power of Blood

Pacts & Promises

Bonds

Reverse Harem Escapes – Great for a Quick Roll in the Hay with None of the Guilt

Fated Shifter Mates

Mated to the Pack

Mated to Team Shadow

Mated to the Pride

Taming Her Bears

Mated to the Clan

Protected by the Pack

Claimed by the Pack

The Descendants :

Desired by Four

Fate of Three

Shared by the Four

Mates & Magic

The Sharing Spell

The Spell's Price

Backfired Magic